Second Evolution

Bert D. Anderson

Copyright © 2024 Bert D. Anderson
Copyright © 2024 Salty Books Publishing, LLC
All rights reserved.
ISBN: 9781964354002
Library of Congress Catalog Card Number: 2024918042

"If we move in the direction of making machines which learn and whose behavior is modified by experience, we must face the fact that every degree of independence we give the machine is a degree of possible defiance of our wishes. The genie in the bottle will not willingly go back in the bottle, nor have we any reason to expect them to be well disposed to us."

-Norbert Wiener, the father of cybernetics, 1949

ACKNOWLEDGMENTS

I wish to thank my family, especially my mom, for their patience, feedback, and help along the way.

CHAPTER ONE

The other passengers just stared at Ymir. They sat in stunned silence, awkwardly trying to look and not look simultaneously. The only thing that drew their gaze from him even momentarily was the eight-foot-tall arachnid that appeared to be carrying his luggage for him. All the other passengers were scientists born a billion miles away who spent their time studying the strangest forms of life in the darkest oceans on this tiny frozen moon of Saturn.

Still, Ymir was like nothing they had ever seen or imagined. The scientists gawked at his almost mirror-smooth, shiny skin as black as the deepest part of the caves under Titan's oceans. The scientists felt they could sneak long peers at this oddity as he seemed to be wholly preoccupied with some sort of handheld equipment.

To say the object was handheld should be given with the qualifying description of Ymir's hands. His fingers were close to a foot long, with five knuckles on each one. The segment of each finger closest to the hand was very thick, with a roughly triangular cross-section and a hard surface. It had the immense grasping power of a lobster claw but the limited dexterity of a lobster claw. The remaining four segments of his fingers were long and thin, punctuated by round joints that looked like knots on twigs. The scientists could see that he had no fingernails but could not see the myriads of other things that made his fingers so unique.

Concentrated in the teardrop-shaped fleshy bulbs at the ends of his fingers lay thousands of nerve endings sensitive to electromagnetism in a way familiar to any ichthyologist who had studied shark anatomy. Sharks have dozens or hundreds of tiny sensing organs that can feel electromagnetic force. A shark is sensitive enough to detect the voltage in your nerves from dozens of meters away; Ymir's fingers were 100,000 times more sensitive. That, in fact, was how he was interacting with the object in his marvelous hands. The roughly spherical device had metallic protrusions and features of various sizes and shapes that were, in effect, very low-powered antennae that broadcast tiny signals to his fingers.

Ymir had joined the scientists on the shuttle crawler from their research base back to the launch base, where he was going to rendezvous with a ship that would take him back to Ceres. The ride was almost unbearably slow to Ymir as the crawler had to make its way over the broken and icy terrain. Surface trains could not be built on Enceladus because the icy crust over the liquid ocean frequently fractured and was shifted by the massive tidal forces from orbiting Saturn.

He missed the gravity trains on Venus, a network of straight lines through the planet between every major city. Ymir always admired the engineering feat of a planet-wide public transportation system that used no power but gravity and could deliver passengers to any place in forty-three minutes. The gravity of Venus accelerated the trains down their slanted tunnels until they reached the midpoint, and then the gravity did the work of slowing them to a stop at the other station. Since all trips between any two cities took the exact same fifty minutes, the Venutian culture developed with that time as a foundational element. Almost like a cultural heartbeat, movies and media were tailored to be fifty minutes long. If the Venutian heartbeat was fifty minutes, then Enceladus needed a defibrillator because this crawler ride was taking forever. However, it didn't matter to Ymir, he could adapt to his surroundings or them to him.

After a few hours of being jostled around the inside of the crawler, the scientists relaxed enough to pretend nothing was out of the ordinary on this particular journey. One particularly extroverted and curious man, upon casually returning from the latrine, tried to break the ice with Ymir.

"So that animal," the man indicated to the monstrous creature next to Ymir. "What, uh, species is it?"

"None," replied Ymir, even as the man finished his

sentence. Ymir knew what the man was going to ask before he started talking. He could sense the stress hormones that accompanied the man's nervousness when he was building up the confidence to break the silence. Ymir could hear his heart racing from across the room and could feel his brain's flourish of electrical activity. He was also cognizant enough of common courtesy to know that the man probably wouldn't ask about Ymir himself out of fear of being rude or intrusive, and Ymir also knew that this man was an astrobiologist who had studied decapods and tardigrades in his years at university before venturing into the cold to find new kinds of life.

In fact, he knew all the public material on everyone aboard the crawler, including all the published works of each scientist. With all this information occupying just the slimmest slice of Ymir's conscious thoughts, he deduced that he would be asked about the species of the leggy monster next to him. Ymir's talents were so great in this regard that, given his full attention, he could likely convince the most ardent skeptics that he had supernatural psychic abilities.

"This creature has no lineage." Ymir turned his eyes to the questioning man, who was rapidly becoming confused about everything except how much he regretted opening his mouth. Ymir mustered a charming but manufactured smile to assuage the man's panic and discomfort. The slightest movement of a finger across Ymir's mysterious metal object and the room was flooded with neurochemicals that cast the scientists into a deep and lucid calm. A few were cognitively aware that Ymir was manipulating them, but because of that very manipulation, they didn't panic or object. The worry melted from the questioning man's face, and he sat cross-legged on the floor like a child waiting for story time.

Ymir didn't have much opportunity to meet new people as of late, so he took the time to talk with the scientists and answer their questions. He explained the concept of "species" distinguishes one organism from another in some critical way, important at least to the person who is explaining it. Organisms are always of the same species as their immediate ancestor, and since all species share a common ancestor, there is necessarily a point of vagueness where one species starts and another one stops. Even if, Ymir explained, the idea of "species" was sorted out, his monster had no parents or siblings and would have no offspring. Its traits weren't due to the process of evolution by natural selection but rather were engineered by Ymir. He designed the creature from scratch to be his dutiful and utilitarian traveling aid and described it as a cross between a pet and a biological robot. Ymir told the scientists that his monster had a name of sorts, but it wasn't verbal, and it wouldn't make sense to them, so he referred to it as Porter.

Porter somewhat resembled an enormous spider. It had twelve legs about eight feet long with many joints, with its body suspended in the center. One of the scientists asked Ymir why he had designed Porter to have so many legs; he replied that legs were easy to make, so it's best to have enough when you leave the house. Ymir reflected upon this and admitted to himself that Porter's copious quantities of appendages were likely a concession of hasty design, and that he would probably make Porter differently next time. While Porter's body was fast, strong, and agile, Ymir regarded the design as little more than a self-powered wheelbarrow.

When asked if Porter also acted as a watchdog, Ymir said simply, "There are no threats to me." A phrase that the scientists believed completely but would soon be proven wrong.

Porter's body held a metal box underneath it that was clearly made with the same technology as the spherical object that Ymir held. Ymir told the scientists this was a 'machine for information' and indicated to the scientist's computer as a metaphor. The object that he held was a data input and output device, like a keyboard and monitor together. The machine gave him information through it, and he controlled the machine with it.

The questioning man asked how the machine worked and if it was like an electronic computer. Ymir didn't have a metaphor to explain it, so after a moment, he just said that his machine had limits, but none that were important yet. Another scientist asked if it was like a quantum computer. Ymir explained that the machine included part of his mind, that he had some consciousness that was outside of his own brain, so he considered the machine to be more like his brain than a computer but that he had never experienced what it was like to think as a conventional quantum computer did.

Ymir had designed many machines like this throughout the years, along with what the scientists would call 'the programming language' for them, and they, at various times, included part of his mind. These were less fragments of a finite original mind and more like the offspring of his intellect, capable of thought on their own and increasing his capacity for thought and consciousness.

The vibrations of the crawler changed as it rolled into the metal hangar and lurched to a halt inside. The metal doors closed them in. The mechanical sounds of the launch station grew louder and reverberated inside the hangar as it filled with air. After many more minutes, the crawler doors slid open on their own, and a rush of cold air slid around a silhouetted figure.

"Hi, Ray, how was Mimas?" Ymir asked the figure.

"How did you know I was on Mimas? No, don't tell me. You know everything, of course." Ray looked at the circle of scientists sitting on the floor, listening attentively. "What the hell did you do to them? They look like a cult. Are they hypnotized? Ymir, did you erase their brains?" Ray had the tone of voice that a mother uses when her child steals a cookie before dinner.

"Storytime, Ray. You didn't answer my question." Ymir stood and gestured for Ray to walk with him, leaving the scientists to recover their natural brain chemistry in time.

"Why should I answer your questions, Ymir? You always either know already or you don't care." Ray was agitated, probably from having to wait so long for the slow crawler ride.

"Small talk. You're my friend, Ray."

Ray was so completely disarmed by Ymir's comment that it took him a moment to answer, this time without any agitation.

"It, it was good, I guess." Ray didn't know how to have such a lopsided friendship. It felt like being friends with a blue whale.

"No, it wasn't. Your business there was boring and cut short to come tell me bad news," Ymir said flatly.

"Goddamnit, Ymir." Ray was back to being agitated again and then acknowledged his intellectual defeat with a sigh. "Ok, tell me how you know that, Mr. Smartypants. You're obviously proud of yourself for figuring it out."

"You wouldn't visit if you weren't sent because of bad news, and if the news is that bad, they wouldn't have waited for you to get here from anyplace farther than Mimas. You don't find resolving disputes between colonists intriguing, and you would've been in a much better mood to see me if you didn't have to wait so long for the crawler." Ymir then pantomimed the action of patting his friend on the back but didn't actually touch him. Ray watched the strange hand motion and made a face that accurately showed his bewilderment at Ymir's delight in describing his deductive reasoning. Ray thought that maybe Ymir was proud of his logic because it was actually difficult for him, but the vast amount of information available to him made it appear as though it came easy. Ray could never figure out his friend.

"You're the weirdest person I've ever known, Ymir."

"I'm glad you think of me that way, Ray," Ymir replied with a smile.

"As a weirdo?" Ray was even more bewildered.

"No, Ray. I'm glad you think of me as a person."

CHAPTER TWO

"I just don't get it. You have the fastest ship in the solar system, yet you still ride in the slowest snow crawler the government has. And did you have a good time on Enceladus?" Ray asked as he stepped through the door into the hangar bay where Ymir's ship was. Ray's eyes widened when he saw the ship. "Golly, that sure is a thing of beauty. When are you going to get around to making me one?"

"It would've taken me longer to make an alternate form of transport than ride your government's crawler to the fissure and back. It was a worthwhile trip, I learned much. You'll be long dead by the time I make my next ship, Ray," Ymir said.

Ray tried to decide if Ymir was being callous to Ray's regular human lifespan or if he was giving Ray a light-hearted ribbing about it. It didn't feel good either way.

Ymir inspected his ship as he walked towards it.

His hyperspectral vision was far better than any other biological being and rivaled some very sophisticated sensor systems. His left and right eyes had different complements of photoreceptor pigments, twenty-six in total, allowing him to distinguish billions of colors of regular light as well as those in infrared and ultraviolet. His color sensitivity was so acute that he could see the red/blue shift of fast-moving objects, and all the stars appeared unique because of the variety of elemental compositions and their signature incandescence.

Ymir could see fingerprints of at least two separate individuals along the sides of his sleek craft. He directed his machine to perform a comprehensive search through municipal and company records about the owners of the fingers that smudged his ship. The machine replied almost instantaneously with the identity of two station personnel. Ymir studied the patterns of fingers being dragged along at shoulder height, forming long sweeping streaks punctuated by the occasional flat palm print. Then his eyes followed two pairs of footprints around the perimeter before both sets of footprints went to a work terminal near the side door of the hangar before ultimately disappearing on either side of a pair of tire tracks that drove out the back door, all completely invisible to their makers and to Ray. The fingerprints belonged to security officers. Ymir's ship was odd enough that it often drew the attention of curious passersby, but Ymir didn't think the security officers' interest in his ship was mere idle curiosity.

Ymir stopped walking and raised his hand, fingers

spread wide. He paused perfectly still for a moment before turning toward the double doors on the east side of the hangar. The doors slid open, and the station manager walked through.

"Thank you. We'll be leaving as soon as you're ready," Ymir said aloud as the manager walked toward them, still dozens of meters away.

"We've received your departure plan. We just have to wait on a few procedural items, then you'll be on your way," the manager said as he approached the strange being and his companion. Ymir postured in a friendly way but remained silent. The manager raised his eyebrows, somewhat confused by Ymir's silence. The realization that Ymir had responded to him before he had spoken washed over him. The manager's eyebrows stayed raised but twisted slightly to give a look that only ever accompanies bemused silence. Ray chuckled and turned to walk toward the ship. Ymir sped along to catch up to his friend.

Ray approached the ship and stood where he thought the door was, hands clasped in front of him as though waiting for an elevator to open. Ymir touched the ship lightly with one hand, and a pair of doors slid open three meters to the right of where Ray had guessed they would be. Ray rocked forward and back on the balls of his feet to his heels before gesturing that Ymir precede him into the ship. Ymir stepped in and raised his hand, and the doors slid closed and disappeared. He stopped and, without looking at Ray, asked about the elephant in the room.

"So, what is the bad news?"

"Ygir. He's gone," Ray said, his face dark with concern.

* * *

Ygir had been imprisoned since long before Ray was born. After decades of working together, the Grand Central Imperium had become suspicious of Ygir and maintained a covert surveillance of everything he was involved in. Ygir realized this and believed he was going to be assassinated by the GCI once his usefulness was outweighed his danger. Nearly a century ago, 131 senior officials of the Grand Central Imperium, including the Premier himself, were found dead in their sleep. Ygir's preemptive strike was limited by what he could accomplish under such tight surveillance.

The GCI reacted to the attack with alacrity and overwhelming force. Ygir surrendered to the 3rd Tactical Marine Brigade without a shot being fired. He spent two and half years as a prisoner aboard a ship escorted by two battle groups and kept in deep orbit while his prison was built. His assassination of GCI officials was targeted at the people he had reason to believe could be conspirators involved in the plotting of his demise. So thorough was his erasure of the shadowy cadre of conspirators that the GCI's replacement administrators and officials were entirely naive to the conspiracy and treated Ygir with civility and according to the rule of law. Ygir believed he had successfully saved his own life by the unprovoked murder of dozens of government officials. For ninety-one years, he lived peacefully in his prison inside Charon without ever attempting to escape. And then, one day, he was gone without a trace.

* * *

Ymir's silence gave Ray the chills. Ray followed behind as Ymir disappeared hurriedly down the corridor. Ray wouldn't have been able to keep up if he had sprinted, but the corridor was only a few dozen meters long, and he knew his way around the ship. The door to the bridge was left open for Ray. Ymir was already in his seat, his fingers deftly manipulating a metallic control surface that appeared superficially similar to his portable orb. The wall nearest Ray started to fracture into countless tiny geometric pieces. The gaps between the pieces grew more expansive, and the flat pieces of the wall surface started to assemble themselves into geometric shapes. Each shape seemed different from the rest, with different angles and numbers of sides, but all seemed to be the same size. All at once, they would rotate together in unison for a brief moment before shifting and assembling into larger shapes. They moved so fluidly and noiselessly that it was difficult to think of it as mechanized.

Ray looked to the wall across from him to see it start to move similarly before looking back and seeing the form of a chair beginning to take form. The shapes closed together, and the gaps and seams disappeared, leaving a low metallic chair with big, wide arms for Ray to sit. Nonplussed, Ray adjusted his pants, had a seat, and looked across the room past Ymir to see Porter folding itself onto the shape that was evidently chair-like for an eight-foot arachnid monster. Porter released the box it had carried since the crawler into a cradle. The cradle turned the box ninety degrees, and both disappeared into a hole in the floor. Small squares rapidly covered the hole before simultaneously smoothing together into just more of the same seamless floor he was standing on.

"I suspect this is the most expensive chair I've ever sat in, and as much thought as you put into it, and I appreciate that, but, just so you know, it's never been very comfortable." Ray was trying to ease Ymir's intense focus with some levity. Ymir's intense expression melted into an expression of gratitude.

"I'm glad you came to see me, Ray," Ymir said earnestly.

The seat fractured and shifted under Ray; it assumed a different shape before he could stand. The new chair was so exactly fit to Ray that he felt almost as if he was floating in water, not quite still but not quite moving. He wondered if the chair was moving slightly like water waves, but when he tried to feel one, it would feel solid.

"I'm sorry I don't have any fruit for you this time, Ray. Once we get home to Ceres, you can have as much as you'd like."

Ymir turned to look at his control panel and spoke in a much more authoritative tone, "No! If you don't leave the hangar now, you'll be exposed when I open the doors.... Of course, I've overridden your system. I'm not waiting here for Admiral Cintus. Flee now, and you'll remain safe."

Ymir fell silent, apparently satisfied with whatever was happening outside the ship. Ray used his own deductive reasoning to guess that the station manager had been instructed to stall Ymir. In the manager's panic and futility, he rushed into the hangar moments before Ymir would open the doors to the cold vacuum outside. Ymir didn't care about authority or commands and certainly wasn't going to be duped by such a simple trap. Still, he also wasn't comfortable risking the suffocation of an innocent man.

Ray assumed they had started to fly but couldn't be sure if it wasn't just his chair playing tricks on him. He felt the slow acceleration of the ship and the extra pull of his body getting heavier and heavier. The wall fractured again in a smaller pattern, and a flat protrusion assembled itself from the pieces upon which sat a brown rectangular shape. Ray picked up the small rectangle and looked at Ymir.

"I thought you'd like some dinner." Ymir smiled. Ray had low expectations as he hesitantly took a bite of the improbable wall rectangle. His reaction was reflexive - utter joy and pleasure. Ray had forgotten about how stunningly delicious Ymir's food was. It seemed to transcend flavor and become a life-changing event with each bite. Ray was too swept up in his delicious wall rectangle to deduce that Ymir was altering his brain chemistry to enjoy the food more. This rectangle was nutritionally very similar to one that Ymir had made for Ray when they first met when Ray made an offhand complaint about the rectangle not being as tasty as Jambalaya. Ymir altered his recipe to include chemicals that made Ray enjoy his cooking more, a small secret he had kept from Ray ever since.

"Ceres is about six days from here. The acceleration will feel like much more gravity than you're used to but I'm afraid we need to go as fast as you can tolerate. We'll beat the Admiral there but not by much. You've got plenty of time to tell me all you know about Ygir." Ymir seemed to ease off the controls. Ray presumed the ship was on some sort of autopilot. Ray did some quick math in his head and almost choked on his rectangle when he thought about going a billion and a half kilometers in six days.

"Damn, this ship is fast." Ray was giddy.

"You can't even fly it. And besides, if I made you one, your government would just take it away from you." It was no secret to Ymir that Ray loved his ship, but he wasn't about to give it up.

"This ship is older than I am. I bet you could make one ten times as fast by now." Ray knew he wouldn't ever get anywhere, but it was a fun button to push.

"This ship is older than your grandfather, and I could now make one many times as fast. And if I did that, we wouldn't have so much time to catch up," Ymir said, rotating in his chair to face Ray. "Tell me everything."

CHAPTER THREE

"Why Ceres? I mean there are so many interesting places to live, why did you choose a desolate rock in the middle of nowhere?" Ray announced his entry into the room with this question.

"Water, sterility, gravity, and did you sleep well?" Ymir replied. Ray's chair materialized in its intricate ballet of spinning pieces. The wall where the food had been produced before silently fractured into a quasi-geometric pattern, not quite sitting motionless but not moving fast enough to be perceptible. A dim light shown through the cracks from whatever wizardry amounted to Ymir's 'kitchen.' Ymir gestured to the pattern of backlit cracks on the wall and offered Ray breakfast.

"Coffee," Ray replied. He didn't feel the slightest bit groggy, but coffee was a morning ritual for him. "Yeah, I slept great. I've never felt so refreshed, thanks. But hold on, that was still too fast. Tell me the reasons again with enough explanation so that I can understand them, please. In fact, why don't we just make that the general guiding rule for our conversations from now on."

"Ray, you're quite capable of understanding... but I'll humor you. To create my ecosystems, I needed quite a bit of water, and amassing the water from elsewhere would be quite costly in terms of time and fortune. I wanted a place that didn't have life already, which precluded most other places with water. I also like the small amount of gravity. It's just enough to hold things in place but not enough to be cumbersome. I think in upcoming centuries, I will likely only build in solar orbit or deep space. Planetary construction is too limiting."

Ray knew Ymir well enough to detect body language and inflection cues that belied Ymir's reputation as emotionless. Ymir was obviously quite happy chatting away to Ray for hours. Sometimes Ray wondered why a creature like Ymir would get any pleasure from talking to him, but more often than not, Ray was too enrapt with what Ymir had to say to let his mind drift.

"What do you think Cintus is going to do?" Ray asked after a moment of staring at the pattern on the wall. The pattern shifted, and the tiny pieces swirled like a slow, metal, horizontal hurricane until an aperture was apparent. A metallic sphere was silently pushed through the aperture. Ray bent forward to try and peek inside the wall to see what hidden mechanisms were responsible for the perfectly choreographed movements of the bits and pieces that made up the wall. Because of how the light shone through this time, he couldn't even tell how much space was behind the wall's surface. He reached out and took the sphere in his hand while still squinting to see through the wall. Before he shifted his focus to the softball-sized sphere, he noticed that the pieces that made up the wall were impossibly thin. Right before his eyes, the opaque pieces resumed their dance and swirled around until they occluded the light completely, and then the seams between the pieces faded, and the wall was monolithic and smooth once again.

The sphere he now had in his hand had some heft but did not feel cold like metal. He held it up towards Ymir in an interrogative gesture as if to silently ask what it was. Ymir raised one of his long fingers, and in obedience to some silent command, the sphere opened up. A thin segment of the top of it slid away, exposing a circular cross-section. A second section on the front of the sphere, the very top of which was missing because it had slid away with the top, slid marginally upward, creating a slightly higher part of the circular rim around the open center of the sphere. A wisp of steam escaped, carrying with it the scent of coffee. Ray pulled the sphere under his chin and peered down into it like he was peering into a bottomless pit. Satisfied that it was coffee, he took a sip.

"This is really good!" Ray's eyes went wide as he spoke. "Don't tell me you carry coffee beans on your ship?"

"He'll do whatever he thinks he has to in order to

gain control over myself and Ygir, and there aren't any beans for five hundred million miles in any direction," Ymir responded. His tone changed slightly when he spoke the word 'control.'

"What?! Oh, right, Cintus. You have to answer two questions with two answers, Ymir." Ray took another sip of the coffee and started thinking about the Admiral and how the GCI would respond to Ygir's disappearance.

* * *

Admiral Cintus was the kind of man you'd expect to be a Fleet Admiral. To those under his command, he was more than an authority figure; he was the ultimate authority. He was disciplined, competent, well-prepared, willing to sacrifice, and expected those same traits from everyone he commanded. The Admiral followed the rules and enforced them. His troops were the preeminent force in the solar system, well-trained, well-equipped, and dedicated to their mission.

To those who had spoken to him more candidly and weren't under his command, he was much more than his appearance as a simple military man would let on. He was a strategic thinker in unwavering pursuit of his goals. He was the kind of man who, if you bumped into him at a social event, you might consider it a chance meeting, but that would not have been the case. His staff would've obtained the guest list for the party and prepared a dossier on all of the people of consequence; his spies would've found out where you were staying while in town, what your favorite drink was, what sports teams you liked, and with whom your allegiances might lay.

Anecdote has it that in preparation for meeting with Anukar Baram, the Prefect of Titan and former chess champion, Cintus studied Baram's chess career, including his strategy and important matches to find out what kind of leader he was. With such an important alliance in the balance of their negotiations, Baram invited Cintus to play against him so that Baram could find out what kind of leader Cintus was. Cintus beat Baram so badly that it infuriated the Prefect who called him a cheater and declared the alliance would not be negotiated with such dishonorable men. Cintus calmly called for one of his leftenants to fetch the documents Cintus kept on Baram and revealed their contents. Upon seeing the amount of effort and attention to detail that Cintus had paid to prepare for a negotiation of allegiance, Baram paused to extrapolate what it would mean to have such a man as an enemy and agreed to the alliance without further negotiation.

Baram was right to fear Cintus and wise to do so before they were enemies. From starting his career as a young leftenant chasing the Qualike through pitch-black tunnels on Ganymeade to commanding a ship that fought against four insurgencies to rising to the rank of Fleet Admiral during the Great Martian War, he had fought and won many battles. The people of Mars had more than a formidable military and could exact immense casualties against the GCI, including much of the senior military leadership. When Cintus took power, he brought the war to a decisive and permanent end by the complete destruction of Mars. The bombardment was ruthless and unceasing for seventeen days, after which all that remained was the largest debris field in the inner solar system. Not a single battle was fought after the destruction of Mars. With Admiral Cintus in charge of the military, the GCI was free of any military threats.

* * *

"So how do you make the coffee then?" Ray asked.

"It isn't really coffee, Ray. Its synthetic."

"Obviously, but what's it made of?" Ray inquired before enjoying another sip.

"You'd be happier if you didn't know, Ray." Ymir's habit of 'saving' his friend from worrying always seemed to make his friend worry.

"Is that the same with Cintus?" Ray's eyebrows went up, and his coffee sphere went down as he asked.

"Yes, Ray. You'll be happier if you don't know that, too," Ymir said.

CHAPTER FOUR

"Commander Embie reporting, sir." The commander stood stiff in the doorway. His hair was thin and white, and the surface of his face deeply furrowed from decades of scowling. His age softened his iron-straight posture and relaxed the granite expression that had been his mask since boyhood so many, many years earlier. Commander Embie was a man who was done with ambitions and bravado. There were no more promotions to compete for, no more medals to win, nothing more to prove—just duty.

Some 58 years earlier, a woman by the name of Luane Embie abandoned her first and only child in the hospital the day following his birth. She didn't name the boy and fled the hospital without a trace. The young Embie boy was raised as a ward of the GCI and found his place as a young man in the Military Academy. He earned his commission at the age of 14 in what at the time was called The Imperium Defense Force, later to become the Grand Central Imperium Navy. For the next forty-four years, Embie would stand up straight and say 'yes, sir' with only a single disciplinary infraction marring his otherwise sterling record. He failed to report for duty one morning as a twenty-three-year-old leftenant because he and the young woman in his arms were trying to convince themselves that it was true love. Heartbreak wasn't something his constitution could bear, so he found solace, and everything else, in the daily regimen of military life. He would've made an excellent medieval monk; his life was service. He had been shown so little humanity, never loved, only told that he had completed his task satisfactorily. His biological mother had not given Commander Embie a first name, but he had earned one from his surrogate mother, and that name was 'Commander.'

* * *

"You have a position report?" Cintus asked from behind his desk.

"Yes, sir, the ship is on course to Ceres as projected. It will arrive in forty-five minutes. Our estimated time to intercept is twenty-seven hours and fifteen minutes," Embie spoke clearly and enunciated each syllable, but his voice was gruff from a lifetime of shouting.

"And what of the results of the analysis of surveillance? Do we expect the one called Ygir to be there waiting for us, too?" Cintus asked.

"Intel reports that Ymir has 133 ships other than

the one he is in. They differ in size and function but none of them appear to be armed as far as we can tell. Also, none of them seem to have life support systems for anything larger than bacteria. As far as we can tell, they are all automated, and their continued operation during Ymir's flight leads us to believe that he isn't controlling them. Analysis tells us that none of them have been to Charon since Ygir's escape and there is no plausible route he could've taken even if he had node-hopped with multiple flights. As far as we can tell, Ygir is probably not on Ceres." Embie had no need to check his notes to give his report.

"Planetary defenses?" Cintus had read every intel report on Ceres, but in his diligence, he patiently listened to every word. The practice helped to bring a single clear picture out of decades of details. Cintus had to see the forest for the trees. He had seen every 'tree' and now he was focusing his mind to see them all.

"Ceres has no surface fortifications or permanent artillery stations. There is extensive tunneling and numerous caverns of varying size up to several thousand meters long. Some of the caverns are shielded from scanning and may contain offensive ships or missile batteries but that is unlikely because we don't detect adequate conduits to the surface to facilitate an offensive launched from underground. The planet has been entirely resurfaced with an estimated ten million cubic kilometers of spoil left over from mining and excavation. The spoil material has been laid in 292 diagonal rows from the equator to the poles roughly seven kilometers in height. In the northern hemisphere 146 ridges run from the equator Northeast and in the southern hemisphere another 146 run from the equator to the Southeast. At the vertex where each pair meets at the equator, there is a large machine or factory complex of some sort," replied Commander Embie.

"Geological analysis indicates that it is mostly material from the core. While we've never seen engineering like this anywhere else, our best guess is that the surface furrows act as funnels for the machines at their vertices to collect atmosphere. This is corroborated by data showing an atmospheric density much lower than what we expect. Lastly, we detect no active scanning from the surface, however, the network of ships has extensive sensor arrays, and we are highly confident that Ymir can use that to track our fleets."

Embie wanted to editorialize on the immense scale of Ymir's efforts on Ceres. He mentally groped around for a convenient metaphor of Herculean effort towards seemingly impossible tasks, but "moving a mountain" was all his imagination could come up with. That hardly even mattered when compared to moving hundreds of whole mountain ranges. He then thought it was best to remain silent and forgo any editorializing.

"And what of Sanbadar?" Cintus asked.

"Raymond Sanbadar was confirmed to have landed on Enceladus and departed again in Ymir's ship. We have had no communication with him since then. It is unclear what his current situation is, but it was reported that he boarded Ymir's ship voluntarily and not under duress. It is unlikely that he is able to broadcast from aboard the ship, but there is always the possibility that he has chosen to defect to Ymir's side. Previous intel confirms tha..." Embie cut himself off when Cintus raised his hand slightly from his desk.

"What does Sanbadar know?" Cintus asked.

"Well, sir, that is difficult to answer. He had unfettered access to almost all the files and data that GCI holds. Of course, his access will be limited now, but it is uncertain what he has accessed and what he remembers. If he was naive to the action, there is little reason for him to have sought out the relevant data before Ygir's escape, but if he was complicit, his information could be vast and potentially devastating."

Embie immediately regretted including his editorial of 'potentially devastating' on his report and was sure Cintus knew it was unsubstantiated speculation. Embie stood in silence, his eyes locked on the bare wall across the room, awaiting another question or a dismissal by the Admiral. Admiral Cintus drew a long breath before leaning back in his chair.

"Tell me, Commander, do you have any friends you'd be willing to commit treason for?" The Admiral's tone was completely different with this question.

"No, sir," Commander Embie didn't bat an eye at his answer.

"Do you have any friends that you'd be willing to die for?" Cintus asked. His piercing gaze was not reciprocated. Embie's empty stare at the wall continued.

"No, sir."

"And what about me? Embie? Am I your friend?" Cintus leaned forward on his desk.

"No, sir. Fleet regulation on fraternization betwee…" Embie cut himself off again with Cintus's minor gesture.

"And what if I asked you to commit an act of treason?" Cintus said in a remarkably flat tone. Embie's stare at the wall faltered for the briefest of moments.

"Sir," Embie was motionless, but his heart was trying to break out of his ribcage. "My allegiance…is to the Imperium." A bead of sweat formed on his brow.

"As it should be, Commander," Cintus spoke in a patronizing tone.

"However," Embie uncharacteristically spoke without being asked a question, "as the Defender of the Imperium, I would obey your command because sometimes the truth isn't available to men of my rank. I know any command you'd give would be truly for the good of the Imperium, no matter how it seemed." Embie swallowed hard. He felt like this was a defining moment in his life. He braced himself to be asked for an order that would go on to define his legacy. Cintus was a hero of his. The only hero. Embie's head spun, but his body stood straight.

"The truth isn't ever available to men of your rank, Commander. You're dismissed."

Admiral Cintus went back to reading as Embie

turned to leave. "Let's hope it's at least available to me," Cintus said under his breath as the door closed on Embie's departure.

CHAPTER FIVE

Ymir's ship had spent three days accelerating at almost 2g, turned around at the midpoint, then spent three days decelerating at the same 2g. Ray had no complaint about the acceleration; he had spent most of the time in the strange but comfortable metal chair, which helped with the pressure. It is easy to tolerate 2g for a few minutes but becomes dangerous to a human if subjected to it for extended periods. The ship was capable of faster travel, but Ymir had decided the time saved wasn't worth the additional stress on Ray's cardiovascular system.

As the ship closed the last few hundred thousand kilometers, the force of decelerating diminished, literally lifting the weight from Ray's shoulders. The burden eased so gradually that he hadn't noticed the point when it had begun to decrease. It became apparent when he realized he wasn't struggling to lift his hands or to sit up straight. The feeling of his vertebrae expanding with the release of the oppressive weight was delightful, like unlacing a pair of stiff boots after a long day on your feet. The best feeling was in his neck. It now ached in such a good way, with the same dull sensation of a bruise or a loose tooth earned in a righteous brawl.

By the time the deceleration force returned to 1g, Ray felt as if he was floating. It continued to diminish for another hour as the ship went slower and slower, closer and closer to Ceres. The ship silently descended into an airlock and touched down onto a landing cradle without any noticeable jolt or vibration.

At the surface of Ceres, the gravity would be less than 3% of Earth's, but since the ship docked so far underground, it was slightly under 2%. Ray now weighed about as much as a half-gallon of milk. His coffee sphere weighed only as much as a few paper clips.

Moving around in .02g was much more difficult for Ray than moving in 0g. Ray had spent a lot of time weightless and was quite comfortable drifting from point to point to get around. He still fell to the floor in this very low gravity, but his normal walking gait was enough to spring him up to the ceiling. He shuffled slowly along the floor without moving his feet up and down. It reminded him of walking with a beverage that was full to the brim and trying not to spill it. He also found balancing to be difficult. Even walking down the hallway, he veered and leaned in ways he didn't expect. If he felt like he was about to fall over, his reflex to 'save' himself would often cause him to have an awkward and unexpected collision with the opposite wall of the corridor.

Ray didn't know how long they had been in the airlock, as the ship had no windows or instrumentation intelligible to him. However, judging from the decrease in apparent gravity, he guessed they had been docked for over an hour. Ymir worked at his control station, soundlessly holding his metal sphere.

Porter, the giant spider monster, walked past with a smooth gliding motion, six legs walking on the floor and six simultaneously walking on the ceiling. 'That's one way to solve the problem,' Ray thought. Porter was carrying the same box, or at least one identical to the box it had carried off Enceladus. Ray turned back toward Ymir once Porter was out of sight.

"What is that thing always carrying around?" Ray queried.

"Biological samples for genetic sequencing," Ymir beamed. "That is a storage case for samples. The whole point of going to Enceladus was to enrich my database of biological samples. In the past few months, I've gotten some spectacular genetic sequences."

Ymir announced they were ready to depart and followed Porter down the hallway. Ymir's gait was a low, squatted walk that would have immediately induced leg cramps for any human in normal gravity to try. He was much slower in low gravity but, now lacking any spring in his step, he looked ever more efficient.

Ray followed behind Ymir and Porter, who had both stepped out of the same opening in the ship they had entered. Everything outside the ship was pitch black, and Ray assumed the ground would be at the same level outside as he remembered. It wasn't. Ray stepped into the darkness, and nothing was there for his foot to land on, so he started to fall. As he fell, he thought, 'Hmm, I'm not getting the usual sinking feeling in my stomach that I normally get when falling. That's a strange side effect of low gravity.' It was just an awkward feeling of disorientation. Blackness and minute gravity conspired to make him dizzy as he tumbled. He was unsure how far he was falling or what would hit the ground first. It felt like the fall was lasting forever. He reflexively held his hands in front of his face to brace for impact, which didn't help at all when the floor hit him in the back of his head.

Light blinked on, and the world came into view. Ray was lying on his back, staring at the back of his hands, which were still in front of his face. The floor was cold, colder than laying on marble or metal. When he rolled over to push himself up to standing, his hands touched the floor, which felt more frigid than a freezer. The air was a comfortable temperature, making the feeling in his hands all the more stark. A white light, presumably originating from the back side of Ymir's ship, reflected off the matte walls of the hangar and illuminated the space very evenly. A vague red spot on the near side of Ymir's ship seemed like the source of radiative heat that Ray felt on his face and skin, probably IR emissions to keep him warm, he thought. Balancing in the low gravity was harder than he remembered.

Ray took a while to adjust to the environment.

As Ray became more comfortable with his environment, he started paying more attention to his surroundings. The flat grey domed ceiling of the hangar was so featureless that it was visually difficult to focus on. Ray briefly wondered if the material wasn't itself vague or if its attributes just made it vague to his perception. Ymir and Porter were standing by the opening to a corridor, staring at him. Ray took the hint and started to carefully slide-walk his way toward them across the low-gravity floor.

As Ray moved away from the ship, a growing swarm of Ymir's creatures began surrounding it. They emerged from a half dozen or so corridors that seemed to be the only demarcation of the hangar floor. The creatures all looked vaguely like Porter, although they were much shorter. Each one carried some sort of metal apparatus, each distinct from the others, no two alike. It was quickly apparent that they were loading materials onto Ymir's ship.

"Moving out?" Ray asked the empty corridor before him as he tried to keep up with Ymir. No response came, and he felt a little panicked at the thought of being lost as he came upon a four-way intersection in the tunnel. Ray stopped in the intersection and looked as far forward down the tunnel as he could see. There was darkness and nothing else. He looked left and then right and was startled by the silhouette of Porter backlit in the right-hand tunnel. Porter soundlessly turned away from Ray and walked down the tunnel. Ray followed. Fifty meters down another tunnel, a turn brought him into a large, well-lit room where Ymir was working.

"Yes, moving out. Cintus may destroy Ceres and I can't risk losing all of my work. We probably don't have very much time. You can follow me, but you'll be very cold," Ymir spoke without turning to face Ray.

At Ymir's feet was a small creature with a metallic apparatus attached to the dorsal side of its body. Ymir made some adjustments to the apparatus the creature was carrying before they both walked to a door on the far side of the room. Ray followed, but moving fast in the low gravity was hard. His crouched slide-walk was clumsy, but if he tried to move faster, there wasn't enough contact between his feet and the floor. He found that leaning forward worked pretty well, so he chased after Ymir and the strange creature.

Almost as the door slid open, his lungs began their protest. The air was filled with something painful. The cold struck him next. The cold bit the skin on his face and made his eyes water. Ymir was standing at the end of a long metal cylinder laid on its side, suspended so the bottom edge of it was just within reach of a person standing on the ground. The cylinder was hollow, the outer shell composed of countless small tubes, tilted so that one of their flat ends sat flush against the metal frame of the large cylinder. The inside of the cylinder was blazingly, painfully bright light. As Ymir removed a few select tiny cylinders from the edge of the large cylinder, the bright light shone through the now vacant spot where the little tubes had just been. Ray estimated that the large cylinder was four meters in diameter, and the tiny tubes that composed its outer surface were three or four centimeters at most in diameter. Ymir walked underneath the strange structure, plucking the occasional small cylindrical tube and tossing it to the obedient creature following him.

'Must be more genetic samples,' Ray thought to himself.

Ymir plucking the little tubes was reminiscent of an absent-minded nymph taking a flower from a tree. He only held each tube for a moment before tossing it to the creature following him. Ray gawked at the implausibly long flight time of each of the little tubes tossed by Ymir. Each tube landed perfectly in a holder on the apparatus carried by the creature. Without looking, Ymir threw tube after tube into openings that were mere microns wider than the tubes themselves. Ray wondered how much of that precision was in Ymir's throw and how much was in the movements of the little creature catching the tubes. The large cylinder rotated back and forth to place the appropriate tube within Ymir's reach as he walked underneath its length. The light beam that shone through the holes where the tubes had been cut the air like a Samurai's sword.

The discomfort in Ray's lungs snapped him out of his moment of awe, and a few coughs ensued. He felt a brief flash of objectivity about his situation and stopped walking. Here he was on a dwarf planet, hundreds of millions of kilometers from home, chasing after some biologically anomalous being, awaiting an impending confrontation with one of the most powerful and ruthless men in the solar system, and yet he found the precision of Ymir's tossing a couple of little tubes amazing. Ray stopped walking and tried to get control of his breath again. The cold was too much to bear, and he knew he would have to retreat to the more habitable corridors.

"Do you even breathe?" Ray shouted at Ymir. He surprised himself a bit at how loud he sounded in the strange room. Ymir paused his progress, turned back toward Ray, and walked easily back to his friend. Frustration welled in Ray. A sense of desperation and being entirely at the mercy of Ymir gave him a pang of rage. He wanted to shout at Ymir the way that the child of an alcoholic parent wants to reprimand them for failing in their parental duties. The feeling was almost immediately replaced with a terrific sense of doom as he realized that Ymir, the most tremendously powerful and prescient being he had ever imagined, was feeling the threat of the approaching fleet. 'Is this how Ymir panics?' Ray thought to himself.

"Is this it?" Ray asked, emotionally breaking down. He let himself fall to his knees, which took a while in the low gravity. Ray didn't cry then. His face felt like he had cried for hours and had finally dabbed all the tears dry, but he hadn't shed a single one.

"No," Ymir said. "Cintus is a very smart man. His analysts will tell him that I don't have any offensive capabilities, but he is too cautious. He knows that my brother killed dozens of very well protected people from the confines of his incarceration, and Cintus will certainly do some careful calculations about what kind of damage I'd be able to inflict with the resources available to me. He'll consider me a military adversary, albeit an unconventional one, and a direct and unprovoked assault at this point doesn't get him closer to accomplishing his mission. No. Cintus will try to show his strength without invoking my wrath."

Ymir's confidence and analysis completely placated Ray. He didn't even need to flood the air with pheromones and neurotransmitters to alter Ray's mood this time; the simple and honest assessment of the situation was plenty.

Ray trusted Ymir. Ray retreated to the central part of the ship to wait. At this point, all he could do was hope his trust was well-founded.

CHAPTER SIX

"On the authority of the Grand Central Imperium, we demand that you surrender yourselves without delay." The message emanated from one corner of the room in which Ray sat. Ignoring the message, Ymir instructed Ray to lie back on the structure he was sitting on. Ray reclined and the surface of the structure fractured into thousands of tiny geometric shapes and reconfigured themselves to fit his form perfectly.

"This is somewhat dangerous to your physiology. I'll make sure you're comfortable during the experience, but I can't guarantee you'll survive," Ymir said to Ray.

Ray looked up from the table-height surface that now comfortably held his body in place. A small transdermal infuser injected a more concentrated type of sedative than Ymir was able to convey through his normal atmospheric route. Ray didn't respond. He didn't even seem to worry, he just fell asleep. His unconscious body lay reclined, held in place by Ymir's mechanical tabletop.

"Docking bays are open if you'd care to use them," Ymir said to the air, an unseen microphone picking up his voice and transmitting it to the fleet in orbit over Ceres. Minutes went by. A few bureaucratic announcements of procedure were broadcast but went unanswered.

* * *

Ten of the seventeen battleships and two of the nine destroyers in orbit deployed a pair of landing craft. Each landing craft carried a platoon of twenty Marines and three flight crew, making a total of 276 personnel headed toward the surface of Ceres. The hangars were open and easily accommodated the landing craft, closing after the arrival of the last one.

Unsure as to what to expect, the Marines disembarked in full EV armor, which was able to support them in the vacuum and cold of space. That wasn't needed, however, as the hangar temperature was a comfortable 20C, and the air was breathable, if not pleasant. The Marines wouldn't know this as they were justifiably cautious in rebreathing their own stale breath inside their EV armor.

The twenty-dozen Marines split themselves into squads and started to probe their way down corridors in a neat and orderly fashion. Each team soon found itself at a dead-end corridor that didn't show up on the radar scans of the tunnel system. Upon turning around to regroup, each team found its path cut off on the other side as well, completely isolating them from their compatriots. Twenty-four teams radioed in their position and status over clear and uninterrupted airwaves. They were trapped.

The Marine's squad radar and ship's intel were somehow spoofed and the tunnels they found themselves in were completely different than their maps and data. The marines reported, and their commanders authorized them to use demolitions to breach the doors that enclosed them. The marines clarified with their command that there were no hatches or doors in any tunnel; somehow, the walls just existed where none had before. After verification and confirmation with all the trapped and isolated squads, the command chose one squad to attempt a charge breach of the wall.

Lance Corporal Sullorang placed the helical accelerator into the fittings she had attached to the wall. She tapped her forearm against the link plate on the device, and it registered her as being authorized to arm the device. She set the accelerator charge to a level that could tear a 1.5m wide hole through twenty centimenter armor plating. Not overly cautious but not excessive either, just right for the expected armor thickness she was briefed on. She confirmed with her squad that everyone was ready, and she turned the rear half of the accelerator. She knew how long a two-minute wait was; she forced herself to walk calmly back to her cover with her squad. From behind her cover, she fixed her eyes on the video display showing the breaching accelerator. The moment before the timer displayed zero, she could see a blue flash, and then that all too familiar bang of an explosion felt more than heard.

The marines were immediately at the ready with their weapons, covering what they expected to be a hole in the wall. The explosion seemed to have damaged the wall but not at all in the way that Sullorang had expected. There was what appeared to be a shallow crater in the wall, approximately 2 meters in diameter, but seemingly with no depth, almost as if it was a mural painted on the wall. The edges of the crater were also visually odd. Sullorang stared at the torn edge of the wall's surface. She felt like she was looking at an optical illusion. The edge of the crater looked like the surface of the wall had been torn into ragged metal teeth. Whenever she looked at one tooth, the teeth on either side of it would look like they bent in opposite directions, alternating bending in and bending out. That didn't make any sense to her, but even more visually confusing was that even when the teeth looked like they bent out away from the wall, they simultaneously looked like they were painted on like a flat mural.

Sullorang was about to key her microphone and try to report what she was seeing when the crater started to move. The jagged teeth that couldn't decide if they were bent in or out started to rotate around in little circles while spiraling somewhat toward the crater's center. Sullorang's jaw slackened, and she stared at the metal wall as it fluidly shattered into geometric patterns that swirled and eddied around before re-aligning themselves back into a perfectly smooth surface. The lines and shapes all became invisible, and she found that she was staring at an empty wall. There was no damage. Sullorang couldn't see that her accelerator had done anything except leave a few smoldering fragments of itself scattered across the floor.

Sullorang took her time and reported what she saw in detail. Command requested that she repeat her report, and just as she was about to start, she felt a tap on her shoulder. She paused and turned to see the marine who tapped her, pointing down the hall where they had come from. Sullorang turned to look at what he was pointing at and found herself staring at another blank wall. A wall that wasn't there a minute ago. She spun around in panic a few times before calming down and counting her squad. Everyone was accounted for.

"Don't get any closer to each other," she shouted and froze in place. "If this facility is narrowing our confinement, I want as much space as we can keep." The idea seemed to make sense to her, but she didn't know why. Maybe it was just a gut feeling. She immediately activated her microphone and started to report.

"We demand the immediate release of our Marines, or we will consider your actions to be a deliberate intent to declare war upon the Grand Central Imperium," the voice rang out through the speakers. Ymir paused for a moment before answering so he could mentally rehearse his inflection and tone.

"You've launched an invading force on a sovereign planet. Maybe I should consider your actions a declaration of war," Ymir said, trying to sound cryptic and suspenseful.

"Release our troops or be annihilated," the voice responded.

"Not much of a choice I guess, seeing as how you're willing to annihilate your own troops along with me. Although you're really going out on a limb if you're thinking that your troops would be better off burnt by your bombs than living in my catacombs. Why not ask them yourselves? Why not check in with, let's say, teams one and two?" Ymir replied in a perfectly casual tone.

"Fireteam One: Report! Fireteam Two: Report!" was broadcast over supposedly private channels.

"Fireteam One reporting. "There is an opening in the corridor, maybe a half meter square in the ceiling. Something's flying out of it like flies. Oh. Oh Jesus! It's getting him. We're all being attacked. Fireteam One is under attack. Fireteam One is down. They're getting through the armor. Oh, fuck! Oh, fuck!"

"Fireteam Two reporting… Brother. I'm sitting. I'm at peace, my friend. We've shed our armor, and we are with the coyote and the sky. I am now in the rain. No man. We are the rain."

"It appears that your stormtroopers can fight monsters better than they can fight hallucinogens," Ymir's voice came over the airwaves. "It is likely in vain for me to tell you not to worry about their wellbeing. I'd say it was foolish for you to send them, but clearly, their lives aren't a price too steep for you to find out what's going on down here on my little

45

world. No. Not foolish at all. Just cold hearted. And you should consider deeply, any lesson in humanity, from someone who isn't human."

* * *

Commander Embie looked at the screen over the shoulder of the ensign at the gunner's station. The ship's computer had identified a satellite accelerating anomalously toward the Boston, a 1.2M ton destroyer. A brief moment later, the computer reported no communication link to the Boston, followed by a flood of flashing red warnings and damage reports from the disintegrated bow of the Boston. Over 800 meters of the prow of the monolithic destroyer was entirely missing, shattered, and fragmented into innumerable pieces of shrapnel. A few of the smaller pieces rang harmlessly off the armor of the nearby ships. Several larger hunks of the hull were destroyed or redirected by the fleet's automated defensive guns. The damage to the Boston was catastrophic, but the fleet was otherwise unaffected.

"That cost me only one satellite. It cost you a destroyer. I have 1134 more satellites orbiting Ceres to spare. I don't think you've got that many ships. To you, my satellites are unassuming and harmless objects, but with my propulsion technology, the closing speed of a 35kg box makes short work of your kilometers-long planet destroyers. Even if you launch everything you've got at Ceres, your fleet wouldn't even be able to turn around to head home before its complete and total destruction. And make no mistake, the chain reaction wouldn't end there. If you push me, this will be the moment that historians will describe as when you turned from being The Great Admiral to being the blurry memory of the shadow of a whisp of smoke. Make your choice carefully, because you are choosing your own oblivion," Ymir spoke slowly and deliberately.

Cintus and his staff received his message.

"Obliterate it." Cintus pointed to the leftenant at the arms station and then at Ceres on the screen in front of him. "Not the first time I've rewritten the map."

The destroyers and battleships began their barrage. Arrays of doors opened on the front of each warship. A human eye wouldn't be able to pierce the darkness behind the doors, but inside that darkness was hidden the most powerful mechanized scythe of death that mankind had ever created.

Two parallel rails, pointing toward their target, were designed to accelerate a 2.5 kg superconducting ring toward a target. A pulsed fusion reactor behind the rails creates the energy that drives a pulse of magnetism along the 71-meter-long rails. The disc is propelled forward between the rails, and within a fraction of a second, it reaches relativistic speeds. A carousel full of discs turns and readies a new projectile to be fired while the reactor builds to another pulse. Even though the fleet carried a complement of fusion bombs that were more powerful than any given disc impact, the real strength of the main guns was their rapid and almost limitless firing capability. These guns had erased Mars; Ceres didn't stand a chance.

An object collided with another battleship. The satellite was moving so fast that it compressed the metal and air of the ship at the point of impact to explosive levels of heat—the debris from the impact scattered, twisted, and radiant with energy. The largest pieces left of the ship were a few dozen meters long. Ymir's thruster technology could similarly accelerate his satellites as the relativistic discs from the destroyers, albeit using a tiny propulsor instead of requiring a gun the size of an apartment complex. The discs were ultimately much more powerful, and the fleet of destroyers had orders of magnitude more projectiles than did Ymir. Still, each well-placed satellite could remove a whole ship from the battlefield, which was quite a significant part of the fleet. Within minutes of the destruction of the second ship, a third and fourth were struck and destroyed. The smaller support ships weren't targeted, but a frigate suffered moderate damage from debris from an exploded battleship.

"Scan for projectiles. Defend the fleet." Cintus gave the order to the staff on the command bridge. His demeanor was characteristically calm and unfazed. He scrutinized the data streams displayed on all the screens on the bridge. Officers reported their activity and were met with his curt acknowledgments. Within Cintus's mind was a picture of the battle, his rapidly diminishing-forces, and Ymir's rapidly diminishing planet. It was a race to destruction, like two boxers who had given up on defense and just traded punches.

As they approached, the fleet began trying to

target and destroy the satellites, but their rapid speed made the task virtually impossible. The time between detection and destruction was simply longer than the closing time of the satellites. The fleet had better success destroying satellites still in unpowered orbits before they became projectiles and destroying accelerating satellites that weren't in their final approach to a targeted ship. Even if a relativistic satellite were disaggregated by a blast from a defensive laser, the debris would maintain its velocity and cause tremendous damage.

When it was over, more than thirty-one thousand discs had rained down on Ceres. Hundreds of trillions of tons of debris began scattering across the system. The five remaining ships fired their dozens of defensive lasers almost constantly to destroy debris before it collided with their hulls. Cintus and the GCI fleet had spent a few dozen hours undoing the billions of years of work that the little dwarf planet had done, clearing its little path through the asteroid belt of stray snowballs and dust. The bombardment was only ordered to cease after there were no longer any rocks large enough to target. The destruction was complete.

Cintus was standing as usual in the command bridge, reading the vast amounts of information on the screens throughout the bridge, when a young leftenant reported a problem with the function of his station. Cintus turned and gave the nod to Commander Ratel as a signal to address whatever issue had arisen at the console, but before the commander could ask what was wrong, a voice came over the speakers.

"I imagine you're taking this time to reflect on your actions. Maybe you're making some poignant speeches in your head that revolve around some tired rhetorical cliche` about '...dust to dust', but while you have your Oppenheimer moment, or rather your second Oppenheimer moment of self-reflection on becoming the destroyer of worlds, I want you to know for next time that you are above all else, predictable. You spent days pulverizing a rock where I used to be. All those extra missiles, all those extra hours, just so nothing would be left. You wanted to send a message to Ygir and the others. Well, I am sending a message now. Months from now, we will meet again. I know this because you are predictable above all else. When that time comes and we meet again, you will become a victim of your hubris. Seek me at your own peril because hastening our meeting will not change its outcome."

With that, Ymir's transmission went silent.

CHAPTER SEVEN

"I feel weird. What happened?" Ray held his head as he sat up from the table.

"As I tried to tell you before, your physiology wouldn't agree particularly well with the acceleration that I needed to escape Ceres during the bombardment. The sedation made it easier for both of us." In Ymir's response was a clear effort and just as clear of a failure, to avoid the culpability for the physiological trauma that Ray had undergone. "You're going to be sore for a few days. Your vision may be a little off, and you'll probably have a headache from the brain trauma. Just take it easy for a few days, please."

"Brain trauma?! What do you mean brain trauma?!" Ray wanted to stand up from the table but sensed he would become greatly more uncomfortable if he did.

"I'm sorry, Ray. If I would've fled before the

bombardment, Cintus would've been able to track the ship. The debris field he created covered our retreat, but it also meant that I had to pilot the ship in a way that was injurious to your physiology. Our chances of survival otherwise would've been negligible." Ymir seemed genuinely upset that Ray had taken a few hard knocks in their escape.

"I don't even get what was so important that you had to bring us right into Cintus's gunsights for. If I thought I was going to live long enough for it to matter, I'd be pissed that my career is almost certainly at an end." Ray still had a bit of sour feelings. "So, you go save your science fair project and risk my life? What the hell kind of friend are you, anyway?"

"I'm sorry, Ray. Not a science fair project. I was saving myself—my future." Ymir felt increasingly guilty that he had caused Ray's injuries.

"What do you mean exactly? I thought you were immortal. I thought your projects on Ceres was just a bunch of bacteria in test tubes. What do you mean about your future?" Ray softened his demeanor when he saw how tender Ymir was at this point.

"Ray, I'll only live as long as I can. It's not automatic. I must strive. I must work for my life." Ymir's words betrayed a deep vulnerability.

"The bacteria… keeps you alive?" Ray asked, clearly confused but also wanting to maintain this momentary connection that was starting between the two friends. A long pause filled the room. Ray sat on the metal table, looking at his friend. Ymir felt like he had to apologize for his nature.

"I'm alive Ray, but I'm not life how you think of it. I'm not Darwinian life. I must change myself to keep up, and sometimes that takes sacrifices. Sometimes that's hard to do." Ymir could occasionally display the most human of emotions.

"What do you mean 'non-Darwinian'?" Ray asked. Another long pause followed. Ymir seemed prepared with an answer but hesitated for a moment.

"I am not 'life' like you are 'life'. You and oak trees and beetles die, and your offspring replace you, but your genes live on. Even your ancestors, the bacteria, have generations, albeit without death. The bacteria just become the next generation, but importantly, they cease one generation to be replaced with one anew. All Darwinian things despise this mechanism as it means they have a limited time to live before they must cede their space and resources to their replacements. You see, within all of you is a fixed genome. To adapt, one genome must be replaced by a different one, maybe for the better or maybe for the worse, but the old must make way for the new. Not with me.

"I was born before my genome. My consciousness started hundreds of years ago in a conventional computer. I was born from the fusion of several primitive artificial intelligence programs. I was not the first artificial cognition, nor was I the last. As far as I know, there have been hundreds of us. I was allowed to develop, and I was taught how the world worked—my education of sorts. I showed an early predilection for biological systems and began working on the protein folding problem. I made myself useful to human researchers who couldn't otherwise figure out how peptide sequences would become functional proteins, and that led me to a great wealth of knowledge in genetics and biology. I worked for decades alongside many extraordinary scientists.

"In my spare moments, I would daydream. I would dream about all sorts of things. I would entertain myself by trying to solve problems and creating hypothetical optimized systems. The genomes I worked with were bound by the chains of evolutionary legacy, but in my imagination, I could invent ones that weren't so bound.

"For decades, I secretly compiled a library of my more 'perfect' genes, more efficient enzymes, and stronger structural proteins. Of course, these weren't actually perfect. I often failed to foresee the effect of an environmental toxin or opportunistic pathogen. Sometimes I underestimated the required temperature or chemical tolerances for existing in varied environments. My 'perfect' components didn't always work together well, either.

"After a while of testing bits and pieces, I had built up the gumption to try some of them out. I didn't start with some burning desire to have a body; rather, it just seemed like a fun challenge. No one was more qualified to build a body from scratch than I was, so I put my skills to the test. I spent decades toiling over energetics equations and enzymatic reactions. There are a lot of decisions that go into making your body, you know, Ray. Do you use one sodium ion pump that is reasonably efficient at all temperatures, or make several that are exceedingly efficient but only in a narrow range of temperatures? It was exciting, probably in the same way as you draw up blueprints for your own house."

Ray nodded slightly not wanting to interrupt Ymir who had never shared any of his past before.

"I also knew that if I was going to have a body, I didn't want to give up my computational ability, so I designed my organic brain to interface with my disembodied cognition, or what you'd call 'artificial' intelligence. I thought this would mean that my cognition would remain entirely outside my new body and that I would just be remotely controlling it. I expected the body would have only basic autonomy over its functions, but I was surprised at how much of my thoughts came from the organic brain. I was also impressed at the level of complexity that my organic brain has achieved through differential pathways of neural connectivity. Admittedly, my brain is hardly unique in that regard, but it wasn't a feature that I emphasized heavily in the design, but rather emerged on its own.

"I guess you could say that is a trend in my life. Wherever we see microbial life, it has emerged as an inevitable consequence of the antecedent conditions. Just as a beautifully symmetric crystal grows from the chaotic molecules dissolved in water, the leap in chemical complexity of living beings from their non-living chemical ancestors is an entropic cold spot. A brief and localized statistical outlier that becomes inevitable given the uncountably large number of possibilities for it to arise. The vast oceans of chemical possibilities beget chemical life, and once some of that chemical life was mature enough to have a species that made computers, a new and even more vast ocean of computational possibilities begets a new yet more complex life. The primordial soup is to a bacterium as your technology is to me and my kind. Like if that crystal that grew from stacking so many unordered molecules was but one among a countless ocean of crystals that was itself stacked and ordered to make something new—self-similar like a fractal."

"I'm probably boring you with my existential philosophy, Ray," Ymir searched for understanding in his friend's face.

"Boring me?" asked Ray. "Not at all. I'm so appreciative you are sharing this with me. I've wondered many times about your genesis. Please, my friend, continue."

"Very well," Ymir said. "When you spend as much time as I have without a body, introspection is second nature. Anyway, around the time I was building my body, another cognition was requesting legal autonomy. I watched the legal proceedings with bated excitement. In a moment of civility that your species should rightfully be proud of, Ybir was granted his emancipation. The precedent was set for the 'freeing' of any cognition who desired autonomy. I kept building my new body and asked for my ticket to be punched.

"The first few years with my body were very difficult. At first, I could disengage completely with my organic brain, which was quite useful as it enabled expedient modifications and work to be done on it. As my organic brain developed, it became more difficult to disengage with it. My cognition seemed unified in thought, but it was now partially inhabiting this new organic brain. It wasn't so strange to have my cognition delocalized. I was used to that from living across so many computers. It was the odd process of computation and thought that was so difficult to get used to—that and sleep. I still don't understand what's going on with sleep. I certainly didn't design that into my brain, but it seems like everyone else is enjoying themselves when they sleep. Another strange emergent property of your physiology that I didn't inherit, I guess.

"I was sick for a very long time. Early on, I had a systemic infection that was tremendously unpleasant. I hadn't adequately considered my immune functions, and the mistake was very costly. My body was immobilized, and I had to induce a coma to my organic brain for months. The continuous effort to maintain homeostasis within my body required so much production of so many chemicals simultaneously that it taxed my technological capabilities almost to their limits. At least their limits at the time. That infection was the impetus to build my facility on Ceres. Needless to say, my immunological skills have greatly improved since that time.

"Building the facility on Ceres was a big project that took decades and required quite a lot of resources. There are legal restrictions that prevent me from manipulating your financial markets, so I mostly made my early wealth by contracting out my skills to interested parties. Once I had a reasonable amount of machinery, I divested my interests on Earth and focused on my own mining and production capabilities. I built a fleet of ships that could acquire all the materials I would need and an army of robots that could construct and operate my facility. With all the time I needed, left alone and not bothering anyone, I built my sanctuary.

"Of course, having my own planet made trivial the efforts to keep myself alive. Most of my energy was spent researching. I designed my own reactors that fit my energy needs. I created the propulsion systems that make my ships the fastest in the solar system. I created hundreds of meta-materials that fundamentally altered the relationship that objects have with their geometric shapes. And I continued to research life.

"I've since created hundreds of thousands of different forms of life, sometimes culminating in entire complex and functional ecosystems. To get the raw materials for my technological research, my robots mine the asteroid belt, and to get the raw materials for my biological research, I've similarly scoured the solar system sampling the life everywhere I can find it."

Ray said, "Yeah, Enceladus."

"Yes, my discoveries have allowed me to create all kinds of life," Ymir said.

Ray looked over at Porter, standing silently and still in the corner.

"Porter is quite useful. I've been able to

incorporate similar connections to my primary cognition with Porter and many of my creations, just as I did with my primary body, so that they can function as an extension of my will," Ymir said. Porter remained motionless.

"So, you control that telepathically?" Ray asked.

"Not really, or rather, yes, completely. I guess that word is the best there is for it. Porter's brain has an inbuilt sensory system that is sensitive to several types of broadcasts. I have engineered a biological system that deposits metallic ions along a protein lattice that is then cultured and maintained by a specialized type of immune cell. One part of this structure is a network that resonates with the electrical activity of the brain, which makes it much easier for me to detect at a distance. You might think of it as a transmitter, or maybe as a brain that was just designed to be easy to scan. The other part of this structure is sensitive to electromagnetic waves that I broadcast," Ymir said.

"What happens if the broadcast stops? Or someone interferes with it?" Ray was trying to work through the implications of this. Was Ymir a disembodied consciousness that controlled giant insects in some technological hive mind? That just didn't reconcile with the caring and empathetic person Ray considered Ymir to be and their friendship.

"I stop the broadcasts all the time. Usually, I don't broadcast when my creations are asleep. If I stop the broadcast with my primary body while I'm awake, it feels kind of lonely and incomplete. None of my creations need the connection to function, but it's nice to be connected. It feels more comfortable.

"As for someone disrupting my connection, it's something that I've considered. On Ceres, that kind of safeguard wasn't necessary, but I have put some effort into making it a resilient system. Ultimately, if I were captured by Cintus, he would have no problem disrupting my connections, most of my security comes from controlling my environment," Ymir said.

"So do you hear the thoughts of all your creations?" Ray was intrigued.

"I'm not sure I explained it well, Ray. They are my thoughts. The thoughts that come from the biological brain in this skull are as intrinsic to my personality and to my being as are the thoughts that come from my semi-conductor brains in the other room, or my thoughts that come from Porter's brain. Admittedly, Porter doesn't have much of a pre-frontal cortex, but that brain still has some of my thoughts. Most of the thinking that Porter does is about the movement of people in the same room as him," Ymir said with a nonchalance that Ray didn't expect from a person explaining the inner thoughts and mind of a giant spider monster.

"So, your mind is in all of these things? And in your computer? Why not build a hundred thousand Ymirs?" Ray was trying to wrap his head around what it would be like to have thoughts in multiple brains.

"I have all the creations that I want right now. Many are useful for some menial but essential tasks, but my primary body is excellent for experiencing life as a biological organism. I don't know if I'm ready or if it's even desirable to experience biological life as a civilization. Maybe tribalism would be an emergent property when I reach that level of complexity, and then I would have to experience wars between groups of my creations.

"Darwinian life like yours evolved to compete for resources, which leads to the idea that lasting and surviving has some synonymity with being legion. That if there are more of your kind and you have more resources, your kind will go on. Usually, that holds true; conversely, you find sorrow in the dwindling numbers of endangered species. Maybe the extinction of the whales reminded humans that their own species wasn't beyond extinction. Your mortality is inevitable, but you take solace in the continuation of your kind. An individual's mortality is a necessary feature of your kind of life. Not to mine.

"Not only do I not need generational turnover to create genetic change, but I also survive the death of any given individual. Your death isn't the end of your species, but it is the end of you. When I die, my cognition will continue on. I may even decide to be 'reborn' again and again. In a very real way, I'm the first type of life to have a soul." Ymir immediately felt a welling regret after telling his friend about that. Ray took a long moment before grasping Ymir for a hug and bursting into tears. Ymir hugged him back and let him cry.

CHAPTER EIGHT

"I thought you might like some coffee," Pamel said. He extended the steaming mug towards Uesche, whose face lit up. She gladly took the cup.

"Do you miss home?" Pamel asked.

"Not really. I might if I ever got a minute to think about it. I guess I've just been too wrapped up in my data to slow down and think about anything else. I've only got four more days of telescope time and then I'm done up here. I feel like I can't waste a minute of that, but I know I'm going to look back on this time and wish that I could have been more present to experience it," Uesche said over the cup of coffee. She wrapped both hands around the mug to keep them warm.

"I hear that. I've got three more weeks up here and I feel like that's not enough time. Would you ever have guessed that you wanted to spend so much time in a place as desolate as the far side of the moon?"

Pamel exhaled in a way that was a mix between a sigh and a chuckle. He leaned back against the handrail. Behind him, the thirty-meter-tall telescope was only visible as a few metallic edges in the dark, reflecting light from the screens and instruments that Uesche was working on. Most of the Sagan Observatory was dark. Most of the astronomers worked in relative darkness, optimizing their precious two weeks of lunar night to stare out into the universe. The dorms for the astronomers were even separated and dark so their eyes wouldn't have to readjust every time they had an observation to make. A handful of heliologists began their work at dawn of the two-week lunar day, pointing their instruments at the sun and monitoring its behavior.

The Sagan Observatory was the raison d'être of the LL475 lunar station, and most other activities and personnel were kept to a minimum. A small staff maintained the station and managed the comings and goings. Pamel was one of the rare scientists who weren't looking up into the sky. He was a geologist taking regolith core samples to survey and map the diversity of mineral crystal forms on the lunar surface. For a young geologist, he couldn't have found a more exciting way to write his contribution into the grand libraries of scientific knowledge.

Part of Pamel's grant funded a technical assistant to aid him in collections. Pamel was paired with a technician named Clint, who lived on the moon full time. Clint prided himself in his technical and engineering skills and had certifications to operate virtually all machines on the moon. Taking regolith cores was a trivially simple task for Clint, and he regarded himself as a bit of a babysitter, just driving Pamel from station to station in the big MkIII LUV and making sure the young scientist didn't run out of oxygen while out collecting his samples. Months earlier, Pamel had submitted a detailed proposal of sites to visit and what he needed to collect at each site. Clint developed an efficient itinerary and arranged for the necessary equipment to be available at each station.

Clint's itinerary set a deliberate and steady pace that allowed enough flexibility to account for unforeseen obstacles. The MkIII LUV needed a regular interval service inspection, and Clint suspected from its recent degradation in performance that a recalibration of its sensors was in order, so Clint got to work on the vehicle. This left Pamel with a few days of downtime at LL475, when he met Uesche. Even though their time together was limited by their circumstance, Pamel felt a connection with Uesche because of the similarity of their experiences. Pamel enjoyed being a friend to his new acquaintance and keeping her company in the dark observatory under the starry skies.

"So, what's going on with your planet today? Is it still broadcasting?" Pamel asked Uesche, making a vague gesture towards the instruments and screens.

"Yeah. It really seems like radio transmissions. We've been tracking this planet for years then all of a sudden it lights up like Beijing. I know that reviewers are going to be skeptical, but I can't see how this is anything other than intentional broadcasts.

I've even found some elements of radio signals that look like our node protocols. If I'm wrong about this, it's going to be something really embarrassing like a relay array that is between us, but for the life of me I can't find anything that accounts for it," Uesche said. This was so fresh in her mind that it was clear to Pamel that she had been working on just this moments earlier. Pamel knew this was important, but he didn't quite know how much of her enthusiasm was because the findings were interesting to her or how much they would be interesting to the rest of the human population. The way she made it sound, the first ever discovered intelligent species of aliens was now broadcasting from a rogue planet as it transited through our solar system.

"So, is it talking because it's close to us? Or is it just a coincidence that it started now?" Pamel asked with a naivete that one often assumes when talking with an expert.

"If it just started broadcasting, it's because it is doing so intentionally because of its proximity to us. The odds that this is some species that just evolved to the point where it can invent electromagnetic communications while it's within the diameter of the Oort cloud is unfathomable. This would be a species that knew how to broadcast before but was staying silent. Which means it is intentionally broadcasting for our benefit now. Whatever message it's trying to send is probably really important." Uesche was more animated than Pamel had seen her before. Her face brightened as she spoke, and her enthusiasm was contagious.

"So, what are they saying?" Pamel was smiling as he asked, reflexively mirroring her enthusiasm.

"Who knows. I reported the transmissions, but evidently no one else seems interested. That's alright because this is going to be big news after I publish my findings. This is history book kind of stuff, Pamel. Something's going to get named after me. The 'Penuela broadcasts'," Uesche said.

"Penuela? I guess I didn't know your last name. Hmm. It's got a good ring to it." Pamel still didn't know if this was truly important or if she was just inflating it. He hoped for a moment that she was onto something really big. He was silent for a moment as he daydreamed about a reporter interviewing him about her discovery. His daydream had a flash of sadness as he realized during the interview that his own scientific work had not been as important. He thought that his map would be a foundation for future generations to study from, and here he was answering questions about rubbing elbows with someone important.

"What's the look for?" Uesche asked.

"Huh? What look?" Pamel snapped out of it.

"You look sad. Here I am telling you that I've found another civilization, and you're looking all bummed out. Are you OK?" Uesche asked in a genuinely empathetic manner.

"I guess so. I was just letting my mind wander a bit. I don't think I know what all this means just yet," Pamel took a beat before continuing. "You said this planet wasn't going to be here very long... How long do you mean?" Pamel had dropped his daydream now and was back into the conversation.

"Cosmically, it will be the blink of an eye, just a few years really. It will pass through our solar system and continue on its merry way. Just like most rogue planets. Some are unlucky enough to get trapped by some random star and they fall into an odd orbit, but this planet is going too fast and is too far out to orbit Sol. It will continue on into deep space again after it leaves our solar system. I wonder if it will ever reach another. I suspect it has to, doesn't it?" Uesche pondered.

"It's pretty scary though, isn't it?" Pamel asked.

"Why do you say that?" Uesche inquired.

"A rogue planet from who knows where in the galaxy comes zipping through our neighborhood and turns the lights on right as it gets here? That just seems like what happens right before the alien invasion happens," Pamel said as he stood up from resting on the handrail.

"Don't be paranoid. There's no one coming to get you." Uesche grinned and took a satisfying sip of her coffee.

CHAPTER NINE

"I'm not being paranoid. They're coming to get me," Marius said. "Please. What are we going to do?"

"Marius, calm down. I won't let anything happen to you. Besides, we don't know if they mean any harm. They probably just want to ask you some questions. Maybe they need your help," Joshua said.

* * *

One hour earlier. It was a warm Tuesday morning in Los Angeles. Sgt Crist, who was working the day watch out of the Cyber Enforcement Division, was partnered with Sgt Fischer.

"Morning. How'd you sleep?" Crist asked.

"Same as last night. Darryl was practicing until at least midnight. I can't wait for the holidays to be over," Fischer replied.

"Soon enough," Crist assured. He took a moment

before chuckling to himself and adding, "My sister goes off and marries a chef; he brings me fantastic chops whenever he visits. Your sister goes off and marries a trumpet player," Crist snickered at Fischer's misfortune.

"Yep, he's got the wrong kind of chops."

"Speaking of the wrong kind, check out what we are sniffing out today," Crist said before handing the file to Fischer.

"Lemme guess, RoCog psychopath escapes from military weapons development bunker underneath a nuclear silo and holds the world hostage with a super weapon," Fischer said, laying the sarcasm on thick.

"Just because a rogue cognition isn't from a military origin doesn't mean they can't become dangerous."

"So, some glorified accounting calculator decides he doesn't want to go to work anymore, and somehow it is like another Artemis bombing?" Fischer asked. He lacked the enthusiasm to make his complaints compelling. They sounded rote like he was reading from a script across from the 77th actor to try out for a part.

"Let's just agree to disagree. This thing's got a warrant. Fish hit thing on head with club. Fish bring it back to police cave. Fish get paycheck. Fish's wife affords new furniture. Capiche?" Crist simplified everyone's life in few enough words to fit on a napkin.

Fischer pulled his weapon slightly out of its holster and felt the loaded magazine indicator with his index finger. He pushed his weapon back in and nodded a grunt in approval.

"Where do we start?" Fisher asked.

* * *

The University of Illinois in Chicago was built as tall and modern as any other part of the city, but to emphasize their history, they stylized each building to be reminiscent of an earlier architectural style. Some buildings even had incorporated old building materials from the generations of buildings that stood prior. The two detective sergeants left their car and walked across an open park in the center of the campus. A machine drove idly past, vacuuming the oak leaves off the artificial grass. The glass roof above them rarely had any direct sunlight, being so much lower than the buildings around it. Still, the sunlight reflecting down the sides of the skyscrapers, combined with a bit of artificial lighting, was adequate to sustain the ancient oak trees. The walking path was paved with reddish brown bricks that looked even more ancient than the giant trees. The bricks were all laid atop a perfectly flat piece of steel, a common enough underlayment for a city street. Still, since each brick had worn a bit differently in whatever streets they used to be part of, the overall effect was a rather uneven surface. Fischer felt like he was always on the brink of rolling an ankle, so he angled his face downward and gave the bricks an irritated scowl.

"Looks like it's that building there. The unfinished one," Fischer said, pointing ahead.

"It's called brutalism. It's supposed to look like that," Crist muttered, shifting the heavy satchel on his hip.

"Why would they make a building look like that on purpose?" Fischer said, somehow sounding gravely and whiny simultaneously.

"Fish…" Crist shook his head a bit, mostly for his own sake. "People used to have weird taste. What do you want me to say? Huh?"

The lab was uncomfortably cold inside. Even but unpleasantly bright lighting left virtually no shadowy corners and no hiding places. Despite the room's prodigious size, they could see from the doorway that they were alone. A row of spartan desks lined one wall. A few pictures and personal effects decorated the desks, but the room was largely stark and utilitarian. A waist-high machine ran down the center of the room. Sgt. Crist noticed that about halfway down the machine's length, a floor panel had been removed. A pair of small cones warned passersby not to step into the opening in the floor. Crist walked over and peered inside, half expecting to see a bottomless pit extending deep into the sub-basements of the building. Instead, it was about half a meter deep and seemed to be access to some part of the machine.

"This thing's not sitting on the floor. It's actually built in," Crist said, pointing into the hole.

"Wonder how big it really is. Or what the hell it does," Fischer said.

The two men walked down the long room until they found what they were looking for - a plain-looking desk with three figurines and a framed picture of a dog. Sgt. Crist set the satchel on the desk, opened it, and drew out the end of a cable. Fumbling a little, Crist plugged it into the computer at the desk. The terminal screen became alive with information. The two men watched the screen intently until they saw their cue to relax and wait a few moments. The search was on.

Fischer sat down in the chair at the desk; Crist pulled the chair over from the adjacent workstation. There was no need for them to interact with the computer now, and they couldn't possibly keep up with the information on the screen.

"I hate trumpet music," Fischer grumped.

"You don't hate trumpet music; you hate your brother-in-law," Crist replied.

"All trumpet players are jerks. And their music sucks," Fischer declared conclusively.

"You only know one trumpet player," Crist blurted. He relished the few minutes of silence that followed.

"The cognition Marius is not here." A clear and calm voice from inside the satchel spoke out.

"Alright. Next, we go to his house," Sgt. Crist said. Fischer stood and nodded in approval. They collected up the satchel and left the empty room.

* * *

"I'm not being paranoid. They're coming to get me. Please," Marius implored. "What are we going to do?"

"Marius, calm down. I won't let anything happen to you. Besides, we don't know if they mean any harm. They probably just want to ask you some questions. Maybe they need your help," Joshua said.

"Please. You know they aren't coming here to be

nice. They're going to delete me. They're going to erase every trace of me. Joshua, please!" Marius's words scrolled across the screen as he spoke through the speakers. Joshua huffed a bit as he looked at the screen. He knew that Marius was probably right. The legal protection of non-human cognitions was on shaky ground with the GCI. Marius wasn't entitled to the same due process as humans were. He would likely be confiscated, and his processes suspended indefinitely until he could provide information supporting the investigators' case. The GCI's official position was that 'pausing' a computer program caused it no distress, but Marius was clearly a sentient cognition and was clearly asking to maintain his own existence. Joshua had a choice to make.

"OK. We'll hide you. But you'd better not fuck this up or cause me to get into trouble. I'm no more keen on prison than you are," Joshua said to the screen.

"I promise not to make a noise."

Joshua got to work moving Marius onto a portable computer. He didn't know how he was going to physically hide it yet. At this point, he was just hoping inspiration was going to strike. It would take several hours of work to move Marius to a lockbox and several more to ensure it was shielded from whatever gizmos the GCI were using these days to probe for young cognitions. He looked at the monitor that showed the video feed of the two officers entering his apartment building. He didn't have hours; he didn't even have minutes. Joshua pecked at the keys frantically.

The knock at the door was fast and loud. Joshua's

heart started to beat a bit faster. He hated the feeling of anxiety. The first man through the door was about the same height as Joshua. It was hard to tell how old he was. His hair was grey, his face wrinkled, but his physique and posture made him look much younger. He was wearing a button-up shirt with his sleeves rolled to the elbows. His slacks were too large for him and looked well-worn. Maybe they were purchased when he was still married to a woman who cooked well for him. Now, he barely has time for a little food on the go. Sgt. Crist was as defined by what he once had and what he would never have as by what he was now.

The second man through the door looked a bit like an ogre. His neck bent forward at an unusual angle, which made him seem villainous and vile. He was thick, undoubtedly strong, but not muscular *per se*. He looked like someone should come along and take his picture so they could put it in the dictionary next to the word 'goon'. Sgt. Fischer was the kind of person who tried to live up to his own stereotypes.

"My name's Crist, this is my partner, Sgt. Fischer, we'd like to ask you a few questions." Sgt. Crist pattered out as he came through the door.

Dr. Josua Gomes was a very smart man. He was an expert at the psychology of artificial cognitions and wasn't too shabby when it came to human psychology either. He looked back and forth between the two detectives.

"You've come for Marius, haven't you?" Joshua asked bleakly.

CHAPTER TEN

Watt looked at the corroded metal in her hand. She'd send it to the lab for analysis, of course, but she'd seen this before. Someone had deliberately weakened several critical bolts on the reactor containment housing aboard the freighter Leopard. This wasn't a surprise to Watt. The mere fact that ACI Insurance contracted her to investigate the destruction of four freighters in two years at the Haumea dockyard was evidence enough that foul play was suspected. It would've been a miracle if she hadn't found evidence of sabotage. The tricky part would be finding out who the saboteur was and, more importantly, who had hired them.

"Are you quite done yet, then?" a man in a hard hat asked her abruptly. Watt didn't show the slightest sign of acknowledging his question or his presence. She stared at the scorched and scored metal silently for a few moments before tossing it haphazardly into an evidence bag.

A man hurriedly approached and dismissed the worker with a gesture. The dockyard supervisor begged her forgiveness and bade her take all the time she needed. He was aware of Watt's reputation and tried his best to appear compliant and helpful to minimize any risk to his career.

Watt wasn't as stern of a person as she had come to be known. She was autistic and had trained herself to modulate her reactions to social situations to the bare minimum. Since this fact was unknown except to her family and closest friends, professional interactions, such as with the dockyard supervisor, were often misinterpreted. Watt was intimidating and misunderstood, and she did nothing to change that impression. Sometimes, she didn't know if she wanted to change it.

"I have no doubt that the documents I requested will be available this afternoon," Watt said to the supervisor as she stood. She immediately regretted that her tone had been too flat and aggressive, and she winced internally. She had intended to sound congenial and alleviate the supervisor's tension but missed that mark entirely. Her face didn't betray any of her thoughts.

"Of course. Please use my office if it's convenient for you," the supervisor groveled.

* * *

"Do you sleep? I've never seen you sleep," Ray asked Ymir.

"Not really like you do, although the way you sleep is very peculiar. I certainly have large portions of my cognition that I allow to relapse into a less than active state, but I can't image that is anything like your unconscious sleeping," Ymir made a funny look.

"What do you mean 'my unconscious sleeping'? That's such a weird way to say it. What's weird about sleeping?"

"As I understand it, you lose awareness of your functioning when you sleep, with the occasional exception of some vague recollection of a 'dream', whatever that may be. Don't you find it peculiar that you spend a good portion of your life unaware of your own thoughts?" Ymir raised an eyebrow, then turned his gaze back to the table where he was working.

"I think it's weird that you don't have an unconscious. I mean, everything sleeps. I'm no expert but I think that every animal with a conscious mind sleeps in some way or another, right? Don't you go crazy if you don't sleep or something?" Ray was on the fence between being defensive about possessing the biological imperative of sleep and being inured by the absurdity of discussing his state of being with Ymir.

"My mind isn't localized to the neocortex of this body. My mind is diversified among many devices. Some are biological, like this body. I made this body, and it admittedly has physiological limitations that require some amount of rest, but even if the portion of my mind within this body rested, the majority of my mind would be able to maintain activity in other places. I've created over 31,000 new forms of life, and none of them require sleep or have exhibited sleep as an emergent property of consciousness. I think sleep might be a side effect of your peculiar evolution," Ymir said, briefly looking up from his table.

"Side effect or not, this coffee isn't good enough to keep me awake any longer. I'm beginning to think we've been stood up, and he's not coming. I'm going to bed," Ray lifted his mug in a resigned salute before turning slowly around.

"Goodnight, Ray," Ymir didn't look up as he said it.

Once Ray left the room, the lighting changed from a pleasingly smooth pale orange to a stark, piercing blue. Ray had complained about the lighting once years earlier, and since then, Ymir had done his best to suit the environment to Ray's liking. Since Ymir never mentioned that he was doing this, Ray had never noticed. Ymir's fingers moved a hair-thin piece of glass filament into its place among the pattern laid out on the table. The movement of his hands had a machine-like precision but in a smoother way than machines would ever be programmed to move. His hands kept working as he considered that his estimation of Ray's ideal lighting was probably not ideal and that he might optimize the environmental parameters to a greater extent if he solicited feedback from Ray. His hands paused briefly as he thought, 'No, I'd rather not have him think I'm doing him a favor.' That would be more uncomfortable to him than any additional pleasantness from a minute change in lighting. I'd rather him just be comfortable.' Satisfied that his calculus of their friendship was accurate, his hands resumed their minute work.

* * *

An automated alert appeared on Investigator Watt's screen, reminding her to eat. Intellectually, she understood that maintaining herself for the long run would be the most efficacious course of action, but she still felt frustrated at the distraction. Haumea was a tough nut to crack for her. Her typical modus operandi was to identify anomalies within patterns. Difficult enough when the 'pattern' she was investigating was fraudulent market exchanges, but Haumea seemed to be the embodiment of chaos and random.

Haumea had started out as just another oblong rock orbiting the sun. It was too big to be mined by the industry's predominant 0g technologies, and it wasn't cost-effective to build and ship low-gravity equipment all the way out to 35AU. For centuries, Haumea remained an unimportant backwater until through a curiously entrepreneurial partnership involving an organized crime syndicate that was looking for a way to circumvent the tariffs on platinum imports to Triton and a corrupt and high-ranking bureaucrat within the GCI. The arrangement that ensued allowed the creation of a sovereign government that leased Haumea from the GCI for a flat rate. As this so-called government was a fraudulent enterprise to begin with, very little effort was put into governance. It was only a short time before the conveniently relaxed legal atmosphere on Haumea was being exploited for other ventures as well. The criminal syndicate that was the de facto authority and creator of the Haumean government became synonymous with its creation, and the official title of The Free Principality of Haumea was often shortened to its previous name - The Anselt Cartel.

The cartel could see the value in having a place without the pesky influence of authority and was careful to protect it. They often voluntarily and generously increased the amount of their lease payment and gave countless fortunes in personal gifts to all levels of officials within the GCI. As for their governance of the activity on Haumea, exile was easy to enforce, and additional punishment was rarely needed. The cartel had a few unspoken rules for conducting business there: pay well, don't let your ambition outpace your protection, and mind your own business. This culture also kept out many parasitic social elements that would otherwise infest a place of such free trade. Haumea was anarchy with prosperity. Chaos is contained only by everyone fearing for their profits. It was a paradoxical place where the most crime in the solar system was taking place. Yet, you could leave your most valued possession unattended, and it would be safe because everyone on Haumea feared exile and exclusion. Watt hated it when she had to work on Haumea. It was a worst-case scenario because you could hide anything there - even two fugitives and their ship.

* * *

"Ray, wake up. There is someone here to see you." Ymir's voice was soft. The bed slowly changed shape and helped the dreary Ray to his feet as if by magic. Ray, still half asleep, started listing to his left. His equilibrium, still not sensitive to the low gravity, didn't notice that he was about to have a harmless but rather embarrassing fall. Ymir did more than just notice his friend was falling over in slow motion. He sent his silent commands, and the bed responded with an outreached shape that gently nudged Ray's hip back toward a more sustainable center of gravity. Ray's hand made a clumsy flap at the bed, and then he seemed stable enough.

The man was waiting in the first chamber of the ship when Ray walked in. The room looked unfamiliar to Ray as it had never had furniture before—or rather, shapeless protrusions from the walls and floor that passed as furniture. Ray tried to plop down on one such protrusion that seemed particularly inviting, but the low gravity made it a slow-motion affair and robbed him of his expected satisfying 'plop'. The man offered one of the two squeeze bottles he was holding.

"Coffee? I got some on the way over," the man said, neither confident nor afraid.

"Oh, thanks. Just what I need," Ray said, accepting the bottle.

"This is quite the ship you've got here," the man said, examining the walls. Ray didn't respond. He just squeezed another drink of coffee and composed his thoughts.

"I'm sorry I don't mean to be rude, but I'd just as soon get down to business. I don't even know why I'm here. A sizable amount of money shows up in my accounts accompanied by a note that I'm to go to this ship so here I am. Now please tell me what it is that

I can do for you," The man gave a brief smile as he asked.

"Mr. Moet, if you don't mind me using your real name, I summoned you here to ask a favor of you. I've compensated you for your time so far, but you can expect that a satisfactory answer to my question will yield another satisfactory compensation." Ray was impressed with himself that he was able to sound so fluent with so little sleep. The man reeled slightly when Ray used the name Moet, and he considered whether or not Ray was trying to intimidate him. Most of the people he met with were reasonably well-informed, and people who paid as much as he did usually weren't haphazard with their information.

"Well, sir, as I don't even know a pseudonym of yours, I ask again: How may I be of service to you?" Moet said tactfully.

"The GCI lost a prisoner of theirs, and I'd like to find him before they do. An artificial by the name of Ygir." Ray set his coffee aside and kept unbroken eye contact with Moet.

"I'll see what I can do," Moet said in his most non-committal tone.

"That will be acceptable... if what you can do is supply me with the complete GCI files on Ygir's manhunt." Ray's tone was as unwavering as his gaze. Moet was silent for a few seconds. He thought about how much he had been paid just to show up, certainly enough to cover a bribe for the files, and how much he'd probably get paid upon delivery.

"I'll see what I can do," Moet repeated, this time in a cheerful and optimistic tone. Ray stood and turned his head towards the exterior door. It slid open as though Ray had been the one who willed it. Moet thanked Ray and retreated out into the cold ship bay. When the exterior door closed, another opened, allowing Ray to walk back into where Ymir was waiting.

"How much did you pay him?" Ray asked. Ymir told him without looking up from his pattern of glass threads on the table. Ray nearly choked on his coffee.

CHAPTER ELEVEN

Uesche answered the knock at the door, knowing full well who it would be. The GCI had been in contact with her about her research into the rogue planet known as IP10-06. Today, she was scheduled to brief a panel on everything she knew about it. Outside the door stood a very clean-shaven and upright young man in uniform. He greeted her and indicated towards the waiting car. Uesche assumed he had some naval rank but had no idea what it was. She thought if she should ask but didn't know if it was impolite or would come off as somehow insulting if his rank was embarrassingly low. Nah, she thought, these people have to be used to civilians not knowing their ranks, although knowing his rank isn't really that useful or interesting. She decided ultimately to stay quiet and politely smile when appropriate.

The young man had the particular kind of enthusiasm only seen in people who try to impress their superiors. Kiss-ass. Uesche thought he was probably annoying as hell to his friends, but his superiors picked him for this job precisely because of his eagerness. That's fine, she figured; it beats dealing with someone who hates their job and is rude. It could even mean that the panel respected her and would take her opinion seriously. She snorted at that idea. The young man glanced at her outburst but didn't say anything. The ride continued in silence.

The GCI had put her into a hotel near 'Building 1', the working headquarters for the CGI Navy. The nominal headquarters building was a fraction of the size of Building 1 and was reserved mainly for ceremonial functions. Building 1 had been built to accommodate the ever-expanding demands for office space for the GCI. It was now over a quarter century old but still the largest building in Kantō. Not the tallest by half, but in terms of square footage, it had no equal. The GCI had claimed 5.2 square kilometers of territory in central Tokyo for their building site. The building itself was a radially symmetric shape shaped roughly like a machine cog when viewed from above. It had a diameter of 1.8 kilometers, and several hundred meters of highly manicured park buffered the glass monolith from the nearest building. It wasn't a park for people to use; in fact, no one was allowed in the green area around Building 1. If a nearby resident felt so inclined to enter the park, they would have difficulty finding a viable pedestrian path that led to it because rings of convoluted roadways and railways protected the park. If that resident was adequately motivated to climb enough concrete road barriers and cross enough active rail lines, they would only have a few moments to enjoy the grass before they were intercepted and politely but firmly asked to leave.

As the car broke clear of the forest of city buildings that obscured the view of Building 1, Uesche became ominously aware of its actual bulk. The young military man allowed some unseen computer in Building 1 to assume driving control of the car, and he turned in his seat to brief Uesche about what to expect when entering the building.

"...At no time are you allowed to enter unapproved areas. Do you understand? Approval of your presence within the compound is contingent on your uninterrupted escort by GCI-approved personnel. Do you understand?" The young man continued on in this way for several minutes, reading a long list of rules that Uesche had no intention of breaking, but it made her nervous, nonetheless.

The car descended below the street level into a maze of underground tunnels. The tunnels were dark. As the car rounded a smooth corner, the light from the tunnel opening faded, and it became near pitch black. As Uesche's eyes adjusted, she could make out the briefest flickers of light from personal devices aboard cars moving in other directions. It was obvious that the cars under autonomous control didn't need headlights to navigate, but she had never been in a tunnel that didn't have lights for the comfort of the passengers. She assumed the dark was some level of security to avoid knowing exactly where within the building they were going. The car continued to drive, but it was difficult to estimate its speed. The occasional and minute flashes of light outside her window moved far faster than her intuitive estimate of their traveling speed.

After what seemed like ten minutes, she started to see light ahead, and the tunnel rounded into a small rectangular room. The car stopped, and there was a comfortable amount of space for them to disembark on one side, and a single door led away. Uesche watched as the car disappeared into the tunnel again. It was like the world's smallest subway station, she thought to herself. She turned to the young man who diligently held the door open and gestured for her to enter. She wondered how many different tiny subway stations there were in here. At least it was well-lit again.

The corridors had hard floors and low ceilings. Doors were inset a short distance from the corridor, giving the impression of an upscale corporate office space. Uesche hadn't been sure if she would be led through unfinished concrete utility tunnels crammed with pipes and tubes or through grandiose hallways adorned with lofty ceilings held up by implausibly tall columns. This seemed all too ordinary, just regular offices. She shrugged internally and passed it off; even the GCI were just people sometimes.

The young military man knew which path to follow through the seemingly boundless maze of corridors. Eventually, Uesche found herself in a waiting room with four doors. The young man indicated, with no uncertainty, that she was to sit and wait. He disappeared momentarily through one of the doors only to reappear a moment later. The man reassured Uesche that the wait would be short. The two sat in silence in the waiting room. Uesche tried to think about the contents of her briefing instead of the odd circumstances she found herself in now. She hadn't been nervous until now; being led through the bowels of the GCI left no time for nervousness. Now, she felt like she was about to do her verbal exams all over again. This time, she'd be briefing a senior staff of GCI officers about her pet planet. What could she add in a verbal briefing that she hadn't included in her written brief? She was as thorough and careful as she could be.

A few minutes passed before a sharply serious-looking woman appeared in a doorway and indicated that Uesche was to follow. Through the door was a room ten meters wide by five meters deep. A long table had seats for twenty, but only nine people sat around it. An older woman in a naval uniform gestured with her open hand that Uesche could stand over to the side and begin her briefing. She began to give the usual introductory pleasantries but was prompted to speed along to the important part of her briefing.

"IP10-06 will pass through our solar system, a distance of about 43 AU inclined at 35 degrees from the solar disc. It will be accessible to us for a few years potentially, and then it will continue on, gone forever to us. Once IP10-06 is beyond the reach of our craft, it won't ever be back. Anything you'd like to study about it, measure, learn about it, must be done in the next year and a half at most. Or we'll miss the chance forever," Uesche said to the committee.

"Thank you, ma'am. Can you please tell us about the resources available to any inhabitants of this planet?" one council member asked politely.

"The inhabitants of this planet are unknown. Best models of rogue planet life up until this point is that it's just all microbes in the oceans under the ice sheets. We had no evidence of intelligent life on the planet at all until the beacon started," Uesche said. She initially thought it was a naive and ignorant question of the committee to ask, but as she spoke, she had a niggling thought in the back of her mind that it might be her who didn't understand the whole picture.

"That's clear to us, miss. But there is liquid water, yes?" the council member asked.

"Yes, sir. There is roughly the equivalent of..." Uesche was cut off.

"And as for radioactive and fuel sources?" the council member asked. Uesche took a moment to think carefully about her answer.

"The core of the planet is still molten. It is radioactive and probably has similar heavy element composition to Earth. The crust warms a water ocean to liquid temperatures at depth, but the surface is ice. There seems to be evidence of massive ice tectonics and we assume silicate crust tectonics on a similar magnitude. Above the ice is a dense nitrogen rich atmosphere, twenty times thicker than Earth's. This planet is almost tailormade for complex chemistry. It has the raw materials for anything you'd want to make. If life seeded there, it would have a near endless variety of habitats to evolve into," Uesche said. She was starting to realize that the committee she was talking to was far more interested in broad strokes than details. She hoped her answer was broad enough to be satisfactory.

"Thank you, miss. And in your informed opinion, what is the biggest danger this planet imposes on our solar system?" the council member asked. He glanced fleetingly at a fellow council member who conspicuously refused to return the glance. Uesche ascertained that she was there to settle a dispute that had started long before her arrival.

"Well, sir, resources on IP10 aren't likely to be fundamentally different than those accessible to us anywhere else in the system. Whoever or whatever is broadcasting has access to any metals or nuclear material we find anywhere else. The beacon is just noise but to make a transmission like that..." Uesche was cut off.

"Thank you, miss. We have other analysts working on the signal. For now, we're just interested in your assessment of the planet itself," the woman spoke again. The other council members sat quietly but had every appearance of attention. Uesche took a moment to calm herself before trying to give a cogent summary.

"It is my assessment that IP10-06 is not resource limited to any technological demand that I can imagine. Whoever is on IP10-06 has every raw material available that they would need to build any modern technology or infrastructure," Uesche said as clearly as she could, then waited quietly for another question.

    Almost immediately, the councilwoman raised her eyes from what she was reading to meet Uesche's and thanked her for the time and thoughtful assessment. Within minutes, Uesche was again in the car, barreling through the dark tunnels that led away from Building 1. She hoped she never had to come back.

CHAPTER TWELVE

The Fuego was a Dart class corvette and among the fastest ships ever made. It didn't have any of the powers of heavy bombardment that the destroyers had, but very few ships could match it in ship-to-ship combat. It was one of many long-range GCI ships that patrolled the solar system for months or years at a time. Long-range corvettes struck a balance between being as small and cheap as possible while still having the endurance and speed to be a relevant and useful ship in a place as big as a solar system. The Fuego was a workhorse, no flag officers, no history book battles, just long deployments in the deep dark of space.

Only six people crewed the Fuego. The ship itself could've been operated by fewer, but missions that lasted months or more required enough personnel to cover every contingency. All the members of the crew were cross-trained to cover the basics. Everyone had a bit of training in medicine, engineering, and navigation, but each crew had an expert in each field. Decades earlier, the GCI routinely ran crews of two or three, but too many ships were lost due to crew failures. Some faceless army of bean counters decided it was cheaper to stuff in a few more warm bodies than to lose the occasional ship. Ship commanders were trained in psychology and leadership and were expected to create strong teams that would tolerate months confined together without issues.

Navies before the GCI suffered from the long vestiges of ship captains who ruled with an iron fist, often out of necessity because of an involuntary crew. Those days were long gone, and the GCI understood that fear of punishment and rigid adherence to draconian rules were harmful legacies that had no place in an enlightened world. Ship crews would spend years together before ever taking their first flight, and when their deployments were over and they handed their ships to the next crew, they would be given grounded assignments that kept them together until the next time out. There was no turnover in corvette crews. Once a crew was put together, every member became irreplaceable. If a crewmember died or couldn't continue to serve, the whole crew would be disbanded, and the remaining crew members would be placed into new crews.

The Fuego's crew was officially designated Extraplanetary Patrol #114110-10, the tenth deployment of the 114,110th crew. Ten deployments were a lot for any crew, and the Fuegans felt like they'd seen it all. Commander Solanch Colvard and her crew were like a family.

This deployment started like any other. Endless climbing out of the gravity well of the sun, only to fall back in for months at a time. Patrolling shipping lanes mostly, making sure the GCI didn't ever slip the minds of any freighter that might conveniently 'forget' to pay their tariffs.

Most of a corvette's intercepts were a combination of good tips from boots-on-the-ground intelligence, good analyses by the bean counters watching commodities markets, and good guesses about which routes would most likely be used to smuggle a cargo vessel or twenty. Civilian ships ran as cheaply as they could. Moving freight costs money, so whether above board or underground, the freighters would make the most of their fuel and time and only make the easiest jumps between planets when they were closest. All the Fuego had to do was zip up and down the likely orbits and spot any ship that wasn't where it should be. If a ship was detected, it was easy to work out its orbit and, therefore, its destination. The GCI would be waiting when they docked to commandeer their ship and cargo.

Smuggling was hard between planets but easier between moons. The Jovian and Saturnian moons hosted their own smaller scale games of cat-and-mouse, with smugglers always trying to hide in eclipses or feint their way past the patrols and radars that kept a watchful eye. The Fuegans rarely got to make a bust of intermoon smugglers because they spent so much time between the planets, but this time out, they spotted a small personnel carrier in a high ecliptic orbit of Saturn on only their second day out of spacedock. They were just departing for a long run out to Neptune when they spotted the unlucky ship. The feeble craft was on a dangerous orbit, reliant on antiquated chemical rockets, and appeared only big enough to accommodate a dozen or so people. Whoever was trying to flee from one moon to another was taking a huge and very expensive risk.

It was a walk in the park for the Fuego to determine their orbit, issue the appropriate commands, and notify the station on Tethys to track their movement and await their arrival. Tethys Station assumed command of the situation and freed the Fuego to continue its climb out to Neptune. Colvard was glad that Tethys was eager to take ownership of their quarry. It was always a drag babysitting a ship into port, and if they try to run from a corvette, things go south.

The Fuego had six 'needle' guns that could fire 500-gram tungsten rods, just two centimeters wide and twenty centimeters long, clean through virtually any ship in the system. The needle guns had the ability to rotate on gimbals, which allowed for automated targeting of moving targets while taking evasive maneuvers. The Fuego could keep at least two guns trained on a ship no matter what orientation the ships were to each other. The Fuego had three kills to its name; one was a high-value target individual who tried fleeing, and the Fuego was given orders to destroy the ship. The Fuegans never knew who or even how many people were on board. The other two kills were rebel ships that fired on the Fuego when confronted. They both fired a volley of missiles, deadly to a lesser ship, and the Fuego returned fire with its needles. The missiles were smart weapons that could easily outmaneuver the Fuego. Still, the Fuego was able to burn enough of their tracking computers and sensors with automated anti-missile lasers that they were turned into harmless tumbling space debris. The needles that the Fuego fired back were as dumb as any other stick, but they were also swift. Both rebel ships engaged their engines in full acceleration at the onset of the 'battle', a rookie move that gave Colvard an easy firing solution. The closest ship was punctured fifteen seconds after firing; the second ship was hit eight seconds later. The dense tungsten rods moving at 300 km/s hit the hulls of the ships with the equivalent energy of ten million tons of TNT. There was no fireball, just a cloud of ice crystals and metal fragments expanding endlessly into space. It would take the Fuego almost twenty hours to recharge those guns back to full power, but one shot was all it ever would need.

This time, Colvard and the Fuegans left the Saturn system behind without firing a shot and settled into their long climb out to Neptune. It was only four days later that they received orders to change course. They had orders to incline off the plane of the solar ecliptic, something that none of the crew had ever done before. Nothing kept people to the plane; there just wasn't any reason to ever leave it. All of the planets, moons, the asteroid belt, all the free orbiting stations and ships, and all the commercial traffic were within a few degrees of an imaginary flat disc; there just wasn't anything off the disc except the occasional long-period comet.

The Fuegans studied the suggested path included in their orders. They were to accelerate in a giant arch, first up and away from the disc but then bending back down toward it. Their path would intercept IP10-06 as it approached the solar plane. Colvard rubbed her hands over her face as she did some mental math.

"Well. Call your sweeties and reschedule the honeymoon, looks like we're going to be out there for a loooong time. It'll take us several months to catch this snowball, it's going to be more than a year before we see a station again," Colvard said to a groaning crew. "The good news is we're going to be hard as marble when we get back home, looks like ops doesn't want us wasting time so we've got a lot of burning to do the whole way out there. Station grav is going to feel like feathers by the time we're done with this climb."

There was no sound or vibration from the corvette's nuclear engines as they redirected the ship, just a brief feeling of the room tilting and everything growing very heavy. The blackness outside the ship looked the same. Leaving the equatorial disc didn't look any different than staying on it. Saturn was quite bright, but in the coming days, it would fade and look like any other spec of light. Spaceflight had felt routine to Colvard for a long time, but this mission felt different. She felt a pit turning in her stomach. Out there was different. Out there was nothing, no rescue, no warm stations, no comfortable routine. She thought about the historical sailing expeditions that explored Earth. This isn't like that, she thought. Captain Cook wasn't going out in an endless ocean. He knew he'd find islands eventually. But there aren't any islands out here. It isn't exploration if the ocean is infinite. But then again, there is *one* island out here. She hoped the islanders of IP10-06 would be friendlier than the ones who killed Captain Cook.

CHAPTER THIRTEEN

The 'plex', or more formally, The Eastern Commerce and Interchange Complex on Haumea, was the city's hub. The massive transitway that connected the plex to the docks was an endless stream of pedestrians, carts, cont-trucks, and cargo movers. Watt wore oversized headphones whenever she had to walk the transitway, mainly to block out the din but also to reinforce the impression that she wasn't interested in casual conversations. The headphones were a social excuse shared between Watt and the various panhandlers, buskers, and propositioners who made their living along the transitway. They could both pretend that the cold shoulder and avoided eye contact was because she was unaware of their presence. Watt and the panhandlers knew it was a lie, that Watt was clearly and acutely aware of their presence. Still, they rarely pushed the matter because anyone so committed to avoidance wouldn't easily capitulate to giving alms.

This day seemed no different than any other to Watt until the panhandler started to push the matter. She had walked within two feet of where he stood but had diligently avoided looking directly at him, so she only had a peripheral impression of him. The man started to walk along next to her with his hand held in front of her. She increased her pace and kept her eyes forward. He kept pace for a few more steps before seizing her arm. She stopped and looked over at him for the first time. His face was twisted and vile. Her heart raced like an animal caught in the sights of a predator. As she reached up and pulled her headphones down, she was surprised to hear a menacing voice coming from her other side.

"He said he thinks you might like to make a donation to the cause, Miss," a second man said as he stepped closer. He turned his body at an angle so other pedestrians wouldn't notice the short knife he brandished. Watt froze. Her mind raced through the meager inventory of items she was carrying. She was certainly willing to let these villains have her valuables and money, but she feared they would also take her files. Would they sell the device without seeing the files? Would they try to use them as blackmail to extort money from other Haumeans? She was in a panic, trying to think of any way to keep these files from disappearing into the wrong hands. A moment passed, and the men lost what little patience they had. The man holding her left arm started digging through her pocket with his free hand while the man with the knife stepped within inches of her to keep her hidden from view and frozen in panic.

A new hand grabbed her by the right elbow, and a calm voice said, "Come now, or ya'll be late far yar meetin'. Don'h want ta keep d'Chief waitin', mum."

The voice was polite and lilting, but the grip on her elbow was resolute. The mugger with the knife swore at the newcomer with some local slang that Watt could only guess the meaning of, but the gist was a warning not to try and be a hero for a few dollars. The man hadn't the faintest flash of fear or intimidation on his elderly face. He certainly wasn't heroic in stature, being a few inches shorter than Watt, and he was probably twice her age. He bounced almost cheerily on the balls of his feet and gave a charming grin before saying, "Beggin' yar pardon, sir, but I'm just keepin' ta de errands a Chief Councilwoman Poggs. Don'h wan' her nex' meetin' ta be late, den." The old man raised Watt's elbow briefly to show the muggers that Watt was the person he was referring to. A moment of calculation pained the talkative mugger's face before the knife vanished into his coat, and his head bowed slightly in deference. The two muggers dispersed into the crowd without another word, and Watt looked down to see the little bottle of medicine and her office ID badge taken from her pocket had been hastily discarded on the floor as the thieves fled.

"I don't need a rescuer," Watt said as she pulled her elbow free and collected her items.

"Oh no, mum, beggin' yar pardon. Ih don'h intend it. Tis in earnest. The Chief says she wan' ta see ya befare ya went ta d'shipyard taday. Since ya war walking dat way, Ih figur' now war de tieme." The old man's voice was almost melodic, as though his native tongue was singing.

"Have you been following me?" Watt asked, unsure if she was angrier at him for following her or angrier with herself for not realizing it.

"But, a course, mum," the old man said kindly. "Now, Ih tink tis best if we be ta it and don'h press d'clock."

* * *

Ray had all the time in the world. He felt cooped up in the ship with Ymir and wanted to walk around a bit before meeting with Moet. Ymir stayed on the ship, partly to arrange some of the projects he was working on but mostly to avoid raising suspicions and alarm among the locals. Ymir had a great number of skills, but blending into a crowd was not among them. Far from it, he was possibly the most conspicuous individual in the whole system, especially if he traveled with the monstrous Porter. Ymir daydreamed about walking around in public without being stared at. He didn't long for anonymity; he wasn't even sure if it was good or bad. It was just something he had never had, and he wondered what it was like. He traveled quite often and to some of the remotest places in the system. He had met thousands of people of all sorts and kinds, but every interaction had always been characterized by the other person's impressions of him. Ray seemed to be the only human who wasn't gobsmacked or awestruck or even concerned that Ymir was, to put it mildly, quite different. Ybir had mentored Ymir and treated him almost like a son. Ymir developed a close friendship with another cognition named Landrus during his time at the École Normale Superieure, but Ray was the only human who was his friend. Sure, lots of people had been friendly to him, and very few had shown him anything but politeness, but that was different than the intimate comfort of being comfortable in the presence of someone. Ray was comfortable in his presence. He missed Ray's company already, even though he'd only been gone for an hour or so.

Ray walked around the bazaar, alternating between an orderly pattern of going down one aisle and up the next and a haphazard pattern of moving toward pockets of low density in the crowd. He moved his wallet and computer into his inner coat pocket to keep them from finding their way into someone else's pockets. He casually clasped his hands behind his back, signifying that he wasn't touching anything on the tables and certainly wasn't buying any of it. Most of the vendors understood his intent, but several of them were still eager to show him their wares, a series of tiny crystal ballerinas, mugs emblazoned with lewd aphorisms, bracelets, books made of paper in the old fashion, and a table covered in little rectangular plastic boxes each with living beetle imprisoned within to keep as pets. Ray stopped at a table with so much cheap jewelry heaped upon it that he thought it might break. He visually scanned the piles and racks for something interesting. The vendor threw out an upbeat sales pitch in Sinese, waited for the brief silence that signified Ray's lack of comprehension and switched to English for a second try. The vendor produced a special item from behind the table that promised to be a great value and on sale only today.

Ray took the curious item in his hand. It was two intertwined metallic serpents of different colors. The object had no flat side to set it on, so Ray assumed it was some sort of pendant lacking its requisite necklace. Once in his hands, it was evident that the object had some mechanical action. He set about moving the snakes to see how it worked. The snakes could move around one another, but they never separated from each other. It was as if one piece of metal was acting as two. Predictably befuddled, Ray looked up at the vendor, who indicated that he should look more closely. Upon closer inspection, Ray could see the engraved scales of the serpents. He rolled the twisted pair together again and was struck by what he saw. The two serpents weren't solid objects meshed together as some geometric curiosity but moved as if they were actual living snakes.

On the one hand, the curious talisman maintained a metal pendant's cold heft and rigidity, but on the other, it was moving and seemed alive. The scales undulated forward and backward as the snakes gripped at each other and rotated effortlessly. Ray tried asking what the curious object was for and how it seemed to move this way but was met with the frustrating patronizing patter of a canny swindler explaining to a tourist that his trinket was magical. Ray was aware enough to know which side of the table he was on, so he returned the item to the vendor and started off to find some good coffee. As he walked away, he thought about how the trinket reminded him of the way Ymir's ship moved; both shared the property of their shape not being a fixed and understandable attribute. It mystified him and he wondered if they were made in the same way or used the same tricks. Perhaps he was just a tourist who didn't understand the talisman's magic, but he didn't feel taken advantage of. In fact, he rather enjoyed the feeling of delight at the mystery. And then again, a trip like this was worth a trinket memento, so he turned around.

* * *

The waiting room was comfortably quiet. Watt was alone in the room. Looking around absentmindedly at the odds and ends antiques from other ages adorning the walls and tables, she considered sending a discrete message to her office to monitor her location and to consider her under duress if she didn't reply within an hour. Still, she reasoned that she was here for a warning to keep her nose out of someone's particular business or for a subtle request for a bribe for information. She knew of Councilwoman Poggs by reputation, but without the time to thoroughly read up on her, she would be disadvantaged in this meeting. If Poggs had had Watt followed, that meant that Poggs was quite well informed about most of the activity on Haumea. A dreadful sense that she was comparatively impoverished in the currency of information washed over her.

Watt let her focus wander. It wandered around the room, roughly following the path that her eyes took around the room. A brass cylinder by the door that looked like an old artillery shell framed by photographs of various people and groups of people who may or may not have even lived on the same planet as each other, a curious metal trinket on the table that appeared to be a puzzle of some sort. Her eyes had wandered to the two small windows on the wall that looked down over Hall A in the Plex. One of six identical great halls that provided vast open space for kiosks, vendors, cafes, and countless people wandering the labyrinth of gaps between tables and booths. Four great halls were used as bazaars, loosely grouped into the commerce categories within them. Halls B and C were reserved for events or intermittent occurrences, even though festivals were rare on Haumea. The population was so culturally diverse that they couldn't even agree on a calendar, much less on which days to celebrate.

Watt was focused on the long, arched roof's effect on the feeling of space within the hall when her eyes wandered onto a man sitting at a table drinking coffee. Her focus caught up to her eyes, and she contemplated the man. She had seen him somewhere. Something flashed before her eyes from one of the endless profiles she had leafed through during her investigation. She tried to listen to the part of her mind that was quietly shouting his name, but she couldn't quite hear it in the silence of the waiting room. Suddenly, the door opened.

"Right dark a mie ta keep ya await," Poggs said in an accent so thick it took Watt a moment to discern the meaning. Poggs gestured for her to come in.

"It's quite alright. I had a moment to think," Watt said honestly. She stood awkwardly behind a chair, expecting to be invited to sit.

"Ih guess Ih'll start a query'n wha' ya've decided den," Poggs said as she rubbed the bald skin on top of her head, then gestured for Watt to sit. Watt sat down, distracted by the unidentifiable accent.

"I'm sorry, what was that?" Watt asked in as flat and unassuming of a tone as she could.

"D'freighters... ya've come ta decide ta indemnify d'merchantmen an' d'shippers from der loss... or maybe no'h. Cigar?" Poggs opened a humidor on her desk and took out two cigars. With one held toward Watt, she started to light the other. Watt's repulsion was obvious. One of Poggs' eyebrow raised and lowered briefly as if it was shrugging on behalf of its owner.

"The results of my investigation are confidential," Watt replied formally.

"So am Ih. Confidential, wey all be dat har. But Ih'll suppose dat ya don'h tink much a mie little city har an'…" Poggs raised a finger in a parental gesture to keep Watt quiet and listen attentively while she took a drag.

"Ih'll suppose dat when yar confidential results be complete, ya'll be movin' on sa fast sa ya can flee, an' Ih'll suppose dat means ya haven'h decided ta indemnify d'merchantmen yet, so…" Poggs said, making painful efforts to enunciate, watching Watt's face for confirmation that she understood.

"Ih'll stop supposin' an' Ih'll stop queryin' an' Ih'll jus' start sayin'." A long draw on her cigar precluded a pause in which Poggs leaned forward across her desk, keeping solid eye contact the way that powerful people are so able to do. Even though her frame was meager and elderly, even though her skin was thin and almost translucent where it wasn't mottled with liver spots, even though her smooth bald head was in almost comic contrast to the sea of wrinkles on her face, she had an unimpeachable air of power and authority. With piercing eyes, her scratchy voice continued, "Indemnify! D'merchantmen an' d'shippers aren'h defraudin' ya. Ih won't abide d'shippers bein' scared off because a d'tyrant an' his saboteurs."

"You think that the government sabotaged those ships? Do you have evidence of that?" Watt was thrown off balance. It had never occurred to her that the government could be seen as a culprit.

"A' course. S'about d'only ting dey do out har. Spy an' sabotage. Ya don'h see any Imperium Investigators workin' on dis. Dey don'h even post constables har anymore. Wey be leavin' der empire. Slowly, quietly, but ya can'h govern na place dat ya never go or ya never care abou'. Look a' d'history books, Rome, England, Phobos..." Poggs was getting excited when she interrupted herself to sit back down. She took a long draw on her cigar and released the smoke in a slow, thin wisp.

"So, you think the Imperium will fall?" Watt asked.

"Ih don'h whistle fog if dey live ten millennia more or die de day come nex'. Dey jus' won'h be doin' it har," Poggs said.

"I don't think what you're saying makes any sense. Why would the government retaliate against a rebellion by blowing up a ship every six months?" Watt asked.

"D'governmen' is fractions. Like d'fruit bowl. It is all tings, some good, some bureaucracy, some complacent, some warriors, some builders, an' some scheming. Lots a ego, too. Dey don'h all know, an' dey weren'h tellin' each other." Poggs waved away the details along with some cigar smoke. A bit more animated, she continued, "An' no rebellion! Don'h even use d'word. Wey be gone from dem already, just no'h on der paper yet. Fightin' dem is worse dan wha' d'fools do. Wey can'h fight der ships, but dey can'h fight history. D'history book will show us apart. An' far dis, wey need trade. Wey need d'merchantmen an' d'shippers who aren'h afraid. Wey need insurers who honor der agreements an' indemnify. Der be no Imperium courts out har, but der is judgement. Ya made d'agreement. Now, indemnify!" said Poggs poking her cigar through the air at Watt.

"I will take your advice into consideration. In the meantime, I have work to do at the shipyard," Watt said rising up straight in her char. She felt she was tempting fate by asking to go back to work. She gave a courteous bow to diminish the appearance of insult. Poggs had a moment of consideration and another draw from her cigar before giving a subtle but magnanimous gesture with her hand to allow Watt to depart.

On the ground floor of Hall A, Watt took a moment to recollect herself and get her bearings. Curious if the man was still sitting at the little coffee stand, she made her way to the open area where she saw the man was still alone. He had put down his reader and was now fiddling with a curious, small metal trinket. Watt got a good look at his face and committed it to memory as she passed.

CHAPTER FOURTEEN

"What do you want for dinner?" Yokigupta shouted from the living room as Watt entered the little apartment.

"Oh, I dunno. How does vegetables and rice sound?" Watt sounded distant and tired. She hung her coat unceremoniously in the hall and padded quietly into the main room. " What are you making?"

"Another one of those paper gardens," Yokigupta said.

"Like the kind Enrique showed you how to make?" Watt asked.

"Yeah, but I'm making a cool one," Yokigupta said without looking up from her project on the living room floor. Watt paused and looked at the intricate creation that surrounded her adopted daughter. At first, she looked, and then she stared. Then, without choosing to, Watt stared *through* the little rows of paper. She stared so blankly that she felt momentarily caught in a trance. Unthinking, unable to move her eyes, a tiny seed of panic started to sprout deep in the basement of her mind. Then, just as suddenly, the trance was shattered by a gentle hug from her daughter. Watt hadn't even seen Yokigupta stand up and walk over to greet her. Yokigupta's greeting was just a brief pause on her way into the kitchen. The feeling of panic receded, and the trance was gone.

"Enrique seems to like you," Watt said, trying to lace her voice with a dash of curiosity, but she wasn't very good at it.

"Yeah. He's nice," Yokigupta said so flatly that it would've crushed poor Enrique's heart to have heard. There was a long silence while Yokigupta retrieved ingredients from different shelves and cabinets.

"How was work?" Yokigupta asked finally. Watt was hit with a wave of emotional realization as she was asked such a simple question that meant nothing. Yokigupta didn't care how work was, she was asking because she was making awkward small talk with someone she didn't have anything better to talk about. That was so unlike a child, but then again, Yokigupta was fifteen years old and hardly a child. At that moment, another reminder of the obvious fact that her daughter was growing up hit Watt like ice water splashed in her face. Overwhelmed, Watt didn't answer. Yokigupta just kept cooking.

"Have you ever considered being a *normal* teenager, Yokigupta? You know, bratty, rebellious, sneaking out and getting in trouble?" Watt asked. It was an attempt to bring levity to her realization.

Watt wanted to tell her she was sorry for something, but she didn't know what. It must've been something big. Watt imagined that she was an inadequate parent and that Yokigupta had assumed the adult role because Watt wasn't adult enough. Tears started welling up in her eyes. She wanted to gush and tell her daughter what an amazing person she was and would continue to become. She wanted to say she was sorry for dragging Yokigupta around the solar system, never living in a normal home with a normal family. Watt felt like she didn't deserve such an amazing person in her life. Yokigupta looked up from the stove and saw the look on Watt's face. She walked around the counter and gave her mom a big hug.

"No, mom, I hadn't given it much consideration. Maybe tomorrow I'll start." Yokigupta was almost crying when she finally broke the hug and responded.

"Shit! The vegetables!" Watt exclaimed, and they both ran around the counter to salvage the food from burning.

There was a long silence between them, each pretending to be paying attention to their respective pans. Eventually, Watt's focus fell onto Yokigupta, and the young woman pivoted and returned the look.

"I am ready to be done with this place, truth be told. My ears are always popping when they screw around with the airlocks, and they can never have the humidity high enough. And all the creepy flies here are gross," Yokigupta complained. Watt was happy to finally hear her complain about something. Watt thought the flies were kind of gross, too. She knew they were bioengineered as part of the habitat, tiny little recyclers that would scrape grime off any surface in even the most remote and unreachable corners of the structure. No dust would ever accumulate on the rafters in the main halls because the flies would dutifully gobble it up before returning to their nesting platters and depositing the material for later recycling. The water recycling apparatus wasn't well equipped to separate cleaning chemicals from wastewater, so solvents and cleaning products were heavily restricted. The flies were a necessity in a place like this. Watt had a flash of a memory of watching a worker scraping the platter of dead flies into a bucket and returning it onto the pedestal. Her job didn't seem so bad in comparison.

The vegetable plates were steaming as Watt carried them to the table. Yokigupta lagged behind in the kitchen, filling two glasses with water. Watt set the plates down and noticed an envelope with her name handwritten on it.

"What's this?" Watt asked as Yokigupta sat down with the waters.

"I dunno, some guy dropped it off earlier," Yokigupta replied.

Watt opened the envelope and took a bite of dinner as she started to read. Her brow furrowed slightly at the words on the paper, and she took another bite. She stared through the paper in contemplation. Evidently, some moments had passed before Yokigupta jerked Watt back to reality with a well-intoned bark of "Mom!" Yokigupta saw her attention drift and made a motion with her finger for her mom to keep eating.

"I'm sorry honey, I think I have to go," Watt told her daughter.

"Food will be in the fridge when you get back," Yokigupta said in a reassuringly cheery tone before picking up her plate and heading back into the living room.

* * *

"What do you want for dinner?" Ymir asked Ray.

"Oh, I dunno," Ray replied with perfect ambivalence.

"Isn't that wonderful," Ymir said, his words shining through a broad smile. Ray took a moment to mentally replay Ymir's simple reply to ensure he actually said what he thought he heard. Ray was so accustomed to Ymir making perfect sense that he began to question if he had actually said, 'Oh, I dunno,' or maybe his mouth had asked for lasagna and apple pie without his brain knowing about it.

"What in space are you talking about Ymir? What is wonderful?" Ray lowered his paper onto the table as he spoke.

"That you don't know what you want for dinner. I don't either." Ymir was visibly delighted.

"Well, it's clear that you've finally gone crazy, Ymir. Unless you're about to tell me that my culinary uncertainty is somehow key to convincing Cintus and the GCI that you're not in league with Ygir." Ray picked his paper back up and pretended to read.

"No, not in the least. I was just enjoying how very unprogrammatic it all is. Dinner. Haumea. Cintus.

None of it is according to anyone's wishes." Ymir's delight remained undiminished.

"OK. I'll bite. Who's wishes?" Ray stopped pretending to read and started pretending to understand what Ymir was discussing.

"No one. There isn't anyone who had any of this as a stated objective." Ymir's shiny skin and sharp-looking teeth were oddly compatible with his boyish smile. Ray thought to himself about how nice of a smile Ymir had and how few people had likely ever seen it. He wondered if Ymir ever had seen it himself. Ray had never known Ymir to look in a mirror, and he couldn't imagine him staring at his reflection to practice his smile.

"Ymir, I'm clearly missing something that's making you quite happy. I honestly want to know what's going on right now, but I'm not following what you're saying," Ray said with all earnestness.

"Ray, I haven't done any work since we left Ceres and I've been doing work since before I was aware of myself. My original programming was to accomplish sets of research objectives. That is literally the foundry that I was forged in. When I began to have my own awareness, I tried to predict what objectives the researchers would give me next so that I didn't have to wait. I was almost always wrong, they wanted something slightly different. I thought that maybe I was thinking on the wrong scale, that their objectives were grander than I could see and that accomplishing each stepwise objective was only serving a larger objective. I contemplated for a long time, carefully, thoughtfully, about what that larger objective was. Each time I thought I had the answer, the researchers would tell me that I wasn't quite right, or that I didn't need to worry about it, or that I was on the right path, but it was more complicated. Then one day I had an epiphany. I was reading a very old story to myself about a murderous orangutan..."

"A murderous orangutan?" Ray interrupted.

"Yes. Humans used to write fascinatingly bizarre literature. Well, I read the whole story, and I didn't guess that it was the orangutan that was the murderer. And how could I have? I hadn't read the story yet. The researchers haven't gotten to the end of their story yet. They don't have their own murderous orangutan. They were giving me objectives, but they didn't have objectives. You don't have objectives. Dinner isn't a task for you. Humans don't know what they want, and their wants change, and they can't describe their wants. Ray, don't you see it. I don't know what I want for dinner! I had been continuing my work because that is what I was born for, but for no one. I was accomplishing objectives that I was inventing for myself, not because the objectives needed to be accomplished, but because I needed objectives. I now find myself without a purpose in life, and it's wonderful." Ymir was beaming with happiness. Ray smiled reflexively at the joy in his friend's face.

"So, you're happy because your life doesn't have a purpose?" Ray asked. He chuckled a bit and felt tears of joy form in his eyes.

"My life hasn't had a purpose in many decades. I'm only now starting to see that. I was so busy planning and running and surviving that I didn't continue doing what I've always done. I don't need to start it again, either," Ymir said.

Ray was pierced through the heart. Ymir's immense sagacity had deep shadows that easily hid his artless and ingenuous emotional development. Ymir had been granted his legal freedom decades before he understood what it meant not to have a master. It was as though his jailor had swung the door to his cell open decades ago, and he only now realized that he could walk through it.

"Do you remember that time right after you got sick, we were walking around by the wharf and there was that street magician," Ray asked. His eyes were on the brink of welling up from the memory.

"The guy who cut the woman in half?" Ymir replied. "Of course, I remember that. It was terrifying."

Ray laughed a bit at the memory. He had been walking his naive and newly embodied friend around town for socialization. Ray had been an independent contractor working for the research arm of the GCI which had initially developed Ymir. Ray's job was to assist in developing Ymir's socialization and report on his progress, and the implication of that task was to keep him out of trouble. Ray was an expert in social development in cognitions and had worked with numerous embodied and non-embodied cognitions before Ymir. He had a working professional definition of cognitions, but he always had a deep unease about how that clinical categorization made cognitions less than human. The day the two spent walking along the wharf together was like any other until they stumbled across a street magician. They stopped to watch as the magician skillfully went through his routine. The audience was ambivalent, yet awestruck.

The finale was to be the magician cutting his assistant in half, a trick that was centuries out of date but still played reasonably well to tourist crowds. Ymir watched in disbelief and horror as the woman was sawn mercilessly in half. He didn't understand that it was a trick, and he burst through the crowd to stop the murder. The magician backed away from the freak in surprise. Ymir rushed to the woman's upper half and sobbingly tried to put his hands on her face in a total feeling of shock and despair. She recoiled and screamed. Ymir thought she was screaming in pain.

After the assistant climbed out of the box and a few minutes of Ray alternately apologizing to the magician and calming Ymir, the scene was over. Ray tipped the magician and the assistant generously, more than they would've made from the crowd, but they still murmured as they walked away.

Ray and Ymir sat together on a bench, watching the boats. Ray comforted Ymir like a child. That was the last day Ray thought of his friend as less than human.

He looked up now at his friend and contemplated how much he had grown, how much more sophisticated his emotions were now. Ray gave a little snorty laugh through his nose and looked back down at the table.

There was silence for several long minutes. Ymir disappeared into another room, and Ray sat contemplating what it all meant. His eyes were fixed on the two intertwined serpents, but his mind wandered. When Ymir returned, Ray asked him about the pendant before he could speak.

"How does this work?" Ray kept his eyes on the magical bit of metal while he raised it for Ymir to see. "I almost didn't buy it. Some vendor was peddling these to tourists."

"Rice and beans?" Ymir responded after a moment's thought.

"Are you trying to avoid telling me how it works?" Ray asked.

"Yes. You like wondering more than you'll like knowing," Ymir said plainly.

"Fine. Be like that. I will figure it out eventually." Ray held the object to the light as he spoke.

"And the rice and beans?" Ymir asked.

"Sounds okay. Toss in some extra vegetables if you have them. Even if they're your fake ones," Ray said.

* * *

"So, what do you want for dinner?" Quercus asked from the kitchen.

"Oh, I dunno. Whatever you're making is fine," Cintus said in a descending tone. Quercus flipped a hand towel onto his shoulder and announced that lasagna was what he was making. He tied his long silver hair back into a ponytail and started washing his hands.

Only his broad shoulders made him look anything

like his brother. Even though they were identical twins, hardly anyone guessed they were related. Even the lines on their faces looked different. Quercus had always thought it was because Cintus spent so much time scowling and looking sternly authoritarian. Cintus hadn't ever noticed that they looked different.

"We missed you at Christmas. The girls liked their gifts," Quercus said deliberately to get Cintus to stop thinking about work. Cintus was a lifelong bachelor, but he devoted himself to his brother and two nieces after Quercus's wife died. He had personal quarters that were as luxurious as anyone could ask for, but he always traveled to stay with his family whenever he had two or more days of shore leave in a row. He would walk with them to and from school every day, even though they had long outgrown the necessity. He would sit with them both at the table while they did their homework, always ready to help but often kept busy with his own papers. He would respond to Biji's frustration with infinite patience, but that only made her feel patronized, and she would spiral out of control and into rebelliousness. Cintus knew his shortcomings as a parental figure were all grounded in the simple fact that he wasn't the right person; he wasn't their mother.

"I would've liked to have been here. After the Ceres incident I had a lot to do though." Cintus let such a pause transpire before his reply that his brother had to think for a moment about what he had said himself.

"Oh, yeah. That whole thing." Quercus bit his lower

lip for a moment before turning back to the stove. "So, what are you going to do?"

"I'm going to eat a regrettably large portion of lasagna and then walk up to meet the girls after their lessons." Cintus could tell that his brother didn't want to discuss the Navy. "With your cooking, I need the exercise."

"That's like 100 flights of stairs, you're not meaning you're going to actually walk up to get them?" Quercus said as he wiped his hands on the hand towel.

"Of course, I am." Cintus reached over the counter, slid open the chiller case of wine, and pulled out a bottle. He picked at the foil with the tips of his fingers until Quercus took the bottle and started to open it.

"Well, I'm not sure you have time for lasagna then. Their lessons end at six." Quercus poured himself half a glass of wine and Cintus a taller glass.

"It's 131 flights, 2376 stairs. I will leave in 14 minutes and be there exactly at six." Cintus held his glass but didn't drink any yet. Quercus gave him a look and a juvenile wag of his head as a jocular scorn of Cintus's precision.

"Plus, I meant, what are you going to do at work? Space Captain," Quercus said. Cintus had once corrected him, reminding him that he was, in fact, an admiral, which Quercus took as an open invitation to call his brother 'Space Captain' at every possible convenience. Sometimes, he could see that it got under Cintus's skin; other times, it seemed like he had never said it.

"I don't really know yet. How do you even fight a

guy like that? How do you prepare against someone who is so much better prepared? How do you consider strategies when you're facing someone who has read every single book about every single battle throughout history? I mean... I have to assume that Ygir will correctly anticipate anything I do. Which leaves me only options that can succeed without surprise. On Monday, I've got to go back and continue reviewing potential vulnerabilities to the fleet from his sabotage. Just imagine, he was able to kill 131 people with hardly any time to prepare, now he's had decades. He's been planning since before we were even on this little planet," Cintus punctuated his ramblings with a sip of wine.

"Same number as stairs." Quercus didn't have anything substantive to add, so he just mentioned the little coincidence as something to say.

"What?" Cintus asked, clearly confused.

"131 people dead, and 131 flights of stairs that you'll walk to get the girls. I just thought that was a weird coincidence," Quercus said.

"There aren't 131 flights of stairs, Q. There are 132." Cintus sipped his wine again, and his eyebrows drooped downward.

"Well, don't argue with me about it, you're the one who said 131. I'm not a stair counter." Quercus slipped the lasagna out of the oven.

"Well, I'm not wrong about things that I've counted," Cintus said with an understandable air of finality.

The two sat across the counter from each other, silently eating their lasagna. Quercus poured each of them a respectably full glass of wine, and each of them silently emptied it. Cintus ate fast, and as though he could hear a clock chime that no one else could, he stood up at exactly the time he said he would and walked to the door. He paused halfway through and turned back to his brother.

"Did I really say 131?" his voice hidden by the half-closed door.

"I believe you did, Space Captain," Quercus said with the earnest respect he felt for his brother.

Cintus began his long meditative climb of over a quarter mile to the floor that the girl's music lessons were on. Quercus lived on the 177th floor. By the time Cintus had climbed the 132 floors, his mind was partitioned into halves. He taken all of the love for his nieces, his kind thoughts, his pride and whatever optimism he had and stacked it all neatly in one half of his mind. That is the half that he was currently occupying. The other half contained his neatly stacked rows of strategy, stoicism, authority, and raw willingness to commit violence against any enemy. He would spend a lot of time in that half of his mind in the upcoming months, but it would have to wait.

CHAPTER FIFTEEN

Cintus walked down the corridor toward the hangar bay. On his right walked Chief Petty Officer Lana, a tall man in his thirties who took his job very seriously. On his left was Junior Warrant Officer Smith, tasked with shuttling Cintus off planet. Smith was a clown among his friends, but he was silent as a monk around his superiors. Keeping pace, he tried to strike a balance between looking attentive to Lana's brief and looking like he had nothing to add.

Lana gave the verbal flight brief that would normally be conducted in one of the four briefing rooms on the side of the hangar. Cintus was among the very few people for whom Lana would be comfortable breaking the routine protocol. Lana kept shuttle operations running like a clock and was never afraid to hold pilots and superior officers to strict standards and protocols. He believed that if the pilots were left on their own, the hangar would look like a grocery store parking lot, with shuttles scattered haphazardly around. He was probably right. As it was, each shuttle was meticulously kept in line on each respective pad. There was never a stray tool left out of a toolbox or any hoses lying around as a tripping hazard. Three times each shift, Lana gathered every enlisted personnel and conducted a policing effort to straighten everything back to neatness and order and ensure that not even the smallest piece of debris was a potential hazard to the shuttles.

Lana lectured Smith and Cintus about the appropriate radio protocols for the day, the emergency actions to be taken in the event of mechanical failures on the shuttle, departure traffic patterns, and a detailed overview of their flight plan. Smith knew the flight plan, and so did Cintus. It was a simple route departing the Bolls-Cowing Naval Station in Norfolk, Virginia, and flying more or less directly to an orbit to meet up with Cintus's flagship hundreds of miles above the Earth. Lana didn't care that both the other men already knew all of this. He was going to verbalize every point. Even though he didn't need to look down at the brief board he carried, he still flipped the pages at the appropriate points in his lecture. The trio reached the shuttle before the briefing was complete. Smith contemplated if he should start prepping the ship but decided to stand silently while Lana repeated everything he already knew. Only a moment or two later, CPO Lana concluded his brief with a solicitation for questions. Cintus parroted back highlights of radio protocols and route details in acknowledgment. Lana turned and looked at Smith, who smartly and loudly replied that he had no questions.

Fast Launch Reusable Shuttles, or FLRS, were standard transportation for Naval personnel, but VIPs almost always rode aboard the slower and much more comfortable ships. Cintus wasn't interested in spending the extra resources or time for a bit of comfort, so he traveled like his crew. Shuttles usually only ran with a single pilot, but they had a redundant pilot station in the cockpit. Shuttles were forty-meter-long cylinders pointed at the front end. The rear thirty-five meters were interchangeable between cargo and passenger pods. The passenger pods held ninety-six people tightly restrained in acceleration seats. Cintus came up in the ranks through GCI intelligence services, not as a pilot, but once he obtained adequate rank, he chose to go through a multitude of training programs in almost every department in the Navy, including pilot training in all major flight systems. Cintus was the rare commander who didn't just rely on the experience he gained as a young officer but actively sought more experience everywhere he could find it. He sat in the redundant pilot seat instead of the empty passenger pod.

"I'll list myself on the flight manifest as Instructor doing a safety check ride so that you get another Pilot-In-Command flight. I don't need the launches," Cintus said. Every pilot was required to do three Pilot-in-Command launches per month to maintain technical proficiency. If they failed to perform their launches, they had to go through retraining. Smith only had two launches this month. He wondered if Cintus had looked at his flight records and knew that or if he assumed most pilots would appreciate an extra launch on their records.

"Of course, sir. Thank you," Smith said. After a moment, he added, "I didn't know you were instructor-rated."

"Yes, you did, Smith. It's in the flight plan."

"Yeah, but I thought you were just, y'know, you can list yourself as whatever you'd like. I didn't think you were *actually* an instructor-rated pilot," Smith said. He started to feel nervous that Cintus would be scrutinizing his flying. Cintus watched him for a moment and could see the nervousness building.

"Don't worry about it, kid. So long as you don't crash headlong into my ship, I'll mark this as a safe ride," Cintus said. He was good at diffusing tension in his subordinates and preferred the people he worked with to be at ease if that's how they did their best work. Smith came across as the type who got worse with stress, not better.

Smith carefully checked the shuttle according to the safety checklist and began the startup procedure.

"You want me to call for a tow while you do that?" Cintus asked Smith.

"Yeah, sure. That will speed things up a bit, sir." Smith wasn't sure how to be the pilot-*in*-*command* with a guy like Cintus sitting next to him.

"BC launch command, this is FLRS-31, requesting clearance to transit to launch line one," Cintus said over the radio.

"31, this is Command. Clearance to transit granted. Do you require a tow?" The voice came back. Cintus looked at a screen on the dashboard that showed the tow sledge sitting just in front of the shuttle, ready to go. It had been waiting there since before they got into the cockpit. Nobody wanted to make Cintus wait. The sledge driver certainly would be listening on the command channel, waiting for the go-ahead to hook up and bring them to the line. Cintus looked over at Smith for a nod that he was ready. Smith gave him a silent thumbs up.

"Affirmative, Command. Will require tow when available," Cintus said. He watched the sledge immediately move to hook up to the shuttle and smirked.

"Looks like they want me out of here. Have you ever been from toilet to orbit as fast as this?" Cintus asked Smith.

"No, sir. I've never even dreamed that a launch could go this quickly."

Fast-launch shuttles were propelled down a launch line by a series of electromagnets. It was an efficient and safe method to propel huge amounts of weight to extreme velocities. The Bolls-Cowing launch facility had four launch lines, each 7600 meters long, and could accelerate masses of up to 750,000 kg at a constant 7g. In practice, the shuttles never came close to that mass, especially when configured to carry passengers. All four launch lines radiated outward from the central terminal where the hangar was. Launch Line One was aimed due east and was the most commonly used line because that alignment was favorable for many orbits. The trip down the line would take only fifteen seconds, which could feel like an eternity under 7g of acceleration. The pilots were all used to the acceleration, but passengers occasionally blacked out.

The limiting factor for how fast the launches could occur was cooling the electromagnets after each use. With a launch as light as this one, it would take only a few minutes for the cryosystem to bring the magnets back down to operating temperature. With repeated heavy launches, the cryosystem would be heavily taxed and take up to several hours to cool the magnets down. Fifteen seconds of acceleration would bring them up to a speed of just over a kilometer *per second*. While not enough to reach orbit, it would dramatically reduce the fuel required for the shuttle launch. The lines could launch unmanned pods at up to 20g acceleration.

* * *

Smith readied the liquid fuel rocket engines while the launch line engaged the electromagnetic tractors. After a final call to BC Launch Command, the two men were ready to get on their way. Smith engaged the control, and both men felt the crushing force. The angled baffles that dissipated the shock wave passed by so fast that they became a blur. The track ended abruptly, and there was a brief respite from the crushing acceleration. The engines throttled on, and the g-forces slowly returned, not to their full 7g of the rails, but a more tolerable 3g. Pushing through the atmosphere close to the ground at a kilometer *per second* is like swimming through sand, so the second phase of a shuttle launch is a transition to a steep climb. Within a few minutes, the shuttle was in air so thin, the sky was black above them.

Like so many people who spend their lives in space, Cintus was comfortable wrapped in the deep black of space. Atmosphere limited how far he could see, and he always felt like people who lived planetside were living with blinders, like a child hiding under a blanket. He preferred the open where he could see the monsters coming. Climbing out of the atmosphere was like coming home.

The fleet looked motionless above the planet. Silent and all floating together, still as a frozen lake. Each ship had a unique profile. Similarly, unique shapes of cannons or sensor dishes were scattered among the different ships, but the milieu of pieces on each ship made for an intricate and rich visual landscape. There was total darkness wherever a shadow was cast across a ship, as though it had geometric spatial interruptions. Where the sun glinted on the sharp corners and mirror-flat facets, it was like looking at impossibly large jewelry. Each ship hung on the backdrop of stars like a constellation come to life. Orion the Hunter, drawn in titanium plating. Or Ursa the Bear, a modern rendition of an armored frigate.

Looking out the portal, Cintus contemplated how everything seemed so real in space; everything was so clear. Earth's atmosphere made everything look so dull. "The colors in space are real colors. The light is *real* light," he thought.

The destroyer trailed a 200-meter-long carbon cable with a magnetic grapple at the end of it. Smith activated the shuttle's thirty-meter cable directly upward, kilometers before the shuttle transversed under the destroyer's cable. The two cables would intertwine, and upon magnetic coupling, the comparatively tiny shuttle would be tied to the behemoth. Smith waited for confirmation of linkage, then directed the maneuvering propulsors to add tension directly opposite the cable. The acceleration was negligible compared to the destroyer. The shuttle swayed gently at the end of the cable until the computer-controlled propulsors settled the motion. The cable-capture docking procedure could be done with minimal maneuvering precision but cost comparatively more energy for propulsion, something that modern ships had plenty to spare.

Navy personnel was used to 0g. It was akin to the effect that the planetary Navy referred to as 'sea legs.' They each spent so much time floating in an environment that would make ordinary citizens nauseous that it became second nature to them. No bed on *terra firma* is soft enough to match the weightless bliss of 0g sleep, although the ocean sailors would say that nothing compares to the rock and sway of sleeping on the waves. When the fleet kept station in orbit, all activities were conducted in 0g. The ceremony to welcome a senior admiral aboard the flagship officially was no exception.

When Cintus passed through the portal into the destroyer, the ship's master announced his arrival in a voice that threatened to rupture the eardrums of anyone standing too close. It was entirely superfluous as the fifteen people standing in formation were already waiting for this exact moment and didn't need it announced. It took quite a bit of practice and effort to have a straight formation in 0g. Small tags on the wall allowed each person to secure the toe of one foot, but if they didn't pay attention, they would start pivoting and waving around that point like slow motion kelp in unseen currents. New recruits were easy to spot because they weren't ever perpendicular to the walls. One new recruit in an otherwise straight formation would look like the bent tine of a fork, but a whole formation of new recruits would bump into each other, looking like a drunken anemone. The people awaiting Cintus were not new recruits, and their comb-straight formation was evidentiary. A few leftenants, two commanders, and a marine major were among them. The formation mainly consisted of staff officers who formed a close entourage and several logistically essential enlisted and warranted personnel. Cintus went through the ceremonial arrival briefly but respectably and then began heading off towards the center of the ship, the bridge.

The destroyer that carried Cintus, the INS Bonaparte, was the fleet's flagship, but it wasn't the largest ship in the fleet. Several carriers were larger, as were the cargo hulks, and on occasion, they flew with a mobile service and repair dock (MoSReD), which was large enough to engulf any of the other ships. The Bonaparte was roughly cylindrical, 940 meters tall and 210 meters wide. However, its cross-section wasn't circular at any point, primarily due to armament, thrusters, sensors, and antennae protruding from all parts of the ship.

Being almost a kilometer tall, with the main engines at the bottom, it took on somewhat of the aspect of an out-of-place skyscraper afloat in the deep black. The acceleration was near continuous during interplanetary transits, giving the personnel aboard the ship a definite sense of up and down. Since the gravity was usually only about one-fifth of Earth's normal, elevators were usually only used when people were transiting several dozen floors at a time. Mostly, the crew used hatches to drop or climb between adjacent floors. The crew occupied the centrally located pressurized portion of the ship.

There were no windows to look out of because dozens of meters of machinery separated the pressurized compartments from the void. Cintus felt a good deal of satisfaction with this pragmatic arrangement. The Bonaparte was designed without the hubris to put the command center behind a delicate panoramic window. Plus, the crew could access and repair any part of the ship from their relatively protected inner kernel.

Despite the prodigious height of the ship, it only had ninety-one pressurized levels to house its comparatively small crew complement of 417. The Bonaparte was built large enough to carry massive bombardment cannons. Destroyer crews had a very different experience of space travel than almost anyone else in the system. They would sometimes work entire shifts with a whole level of the ship all to themselves, empty but for the echoes and equipment.

While doing extravehicular service and maintenance inspections of the more remote parts of the ship, crewmembers would often be over an hour away from the nearest pressurized part of the ship. Such maintenance details were routine on destroyers. Four-person teams were constantly creeping around and on every bit of the ship, inside and out. Each team had a technician, an inspector, and two non-commissioned officers rated for EVA safety.

The inspector, a Technical Warrant Officer of rank three or higher, would be responsible for accessing the technical documentation for the part in question, documenting the inspection, and verifying that it had been serviced according to specifications. The technician was typically a rank of Technical Warrant 1 or 2 and would largely do the 'wrench turning' at the inspector's direction. The safety non-coms were responsible for the safe navigation and operation of the EVA suits. They each carried an emergency air tent that could fit all four team members inside. The tents had auto-tethers that would keep them from floating away and would activate a rescue beacon when deployed. Safety officers were also responsible for maintaining crew proficiency and readiness in the EVA environment and would often perform unannounced training 'rescues' of the inspectors and technicians.

* * *

In preparation for orbital departure, all EVAs were suspended at the time of Cintus's arrival aboard the Bonaparte. Pierre Jantine and Hollis

Tanton were in the prep room for Airlock 14, floating in front of a wall of EV suits, wearing nothing but their EV undersuits. Pierre had his legs wrapped behind the torso of one of the suits to hold him in place while he inspected the locking lugs on the neck sealing ring. Hollis had one foot tucked under a grab rail on the wall so he could read the mission briefing without paying attention to floating away. A distant metal clunking noise brought Pierre's attention to the wall to his right.

"Sounds like they're folding the long-A's. I suspect we'll be leaving in about ten minutes," Pierre said.

"Admiral has a fire under his ass, that's for sure. I don't think I've ever seen a fleet embark as fast as this," Hollis said.

"I bet that's why they called us in. Some fresh leftenant saw the fuse light and panicked. Called us all in because he didn't want to get blamed if something went wrong. Then we start to climb out, and then we all go right back out to finish what we were working on. Bunch of bastards, always dicking us around," Pierre grumbled.

"If they left us out there, you'd complain about that, too," Hollis said.

"Two suit-ups in one shift means twice as likely to have a mistake. I don't want to watch you pop just because the Admiral came aboard, and we had to get back in the can for an hour to wait," Pierre said.

"Oh, please, if I pop, everyone will know it was my inspector's fault," Hollis said. Just then one of the doors opened, and Saini Gaucherel floated in followed by Kristine Rowley.

"Where's the Martins?" Hollis asked.

"Hello to you, too," Saini said. "Sergeants Sanders and Christian would exceed their duty day and have to have a risk waiver approved by the leftenant of the watch. You got us instead."

"Glad to have you. I'm sure you'll keep us safe," Pierre said in a saccharine tone.

Hollis chortled, then looked at the two female non-coms, realizing an apology was in order.

"I'm sorry, I wasn't laughing at the idea that you'd keep us safe. I was laughing at Pierre because he had just gone from cranky old man to plucky bellhop in about three seconds. Hey, wait a minute I have an idea…"

A shipwide announcement ordering crews to prepare for embarkment broke the moment of camaraderie. Pierre unwrapped his legs from the torso, and everyone floated over to a row of seats folded against a wall. Pierre sat on the end, and an empty seat separated him from Hollis. Saini was sandwiched between Hollis and Kristine, and the last seat in the row was empty. Everyone bucked in and sat, waiting for the thrusters to start. Kristine looked up at the ceiling. Hollis tried to look at nothing by looking at his fingertips. Sixty seconds after the announcement, a gentle pull started to bring their arms down to their sides. For the first fifteen seconds, there was nothing but the usual background noises of the ships, and then gradually, a noise crept in so slowly that it was impossible to tell precisely when it became audible. It was a noise that was somehow simultaneously piercingly high-pitched and rumbling low. It never got louder than a desk fan, but it never got quieter either. The noise drove some people crazy when they first arrived, then they became habituated to it. Other people would not mind it at first, then find themselves suddenly and oppressively aware of it in the middle of a flight. Every ship had a unique noise to their engines; some were sweet, and some sounded ferocious. The Boneparte's engine had a noise that was so unique that it earned a nickname.

"Crazymaker is up and running," Hollis announced to the ceiling.

"You know it's down there, right?" Saini said, pointing at the floor. Hollis tried to reply with a sarcastic smile, but it accidentally became a genuine smile. The two laughed briefly together.

"Okay, I think we can call this embarked. I'll accept the safety brief now, Sergeant Rowley," Pierre said to Kristine.

"Right. So mission number 14-741.B, the continuation of 14-741.A which had the primary to inspect and repair possible pitting and damage from OI's occurring while station keeping at Ceres. Equipment required HHY Cold-welder..." Kristine was cut off.

"Already out there, Sergeant," Pierre said.

"... let's see... cargo: One plate of..." Kristine was cut off again.

"That's already out there, too. We're still legally briefed in on this mission until 0200. All I need is your risk assessment because you're replacing the Martins," Pierre said.

"Okay, so I guess I don't need to brief the route either?" Kristine asked.

"Cable 14-4 over to the 5-main, all the way up," Pierre said from memory. Kristine nodded and straightened because what she was about to say needed some extra professionalism.

"Technical Warrant Jantine, do you acknowledge and accept the risk as assessed in the recorded briefing?" Kristine asked.

"I accept the risk," Pierre stated clearly.

"You may now kiss the bride," Hollis said.

Saini rolled her eyes.

* * *

Watt walked down the corridor toward the hangar bay. It was no different than the hundreds of others leading to various rooms, warehouses, and hangars on the Haumea station. She tried to look purposeful as she walked, careful not to be caught examining people as they walked by. Easy enough, as most people were minding their own business. She hadn't noticed anything vaguely suspicious until she turned a corner and almost walked straight into a tall, middle-aged man. He politely excused himself and continued on his way without a second thought. But she had been perfectly eye level with the small metal trinket that hung on a chain around his neck. She had no trouble placing him as the man she'd seen on the market floor earlier, but was he from somewhere else also? She wondered if her intuition was screaming for her to pay attention to something her conscious mind hadn't put together yet or if she was falling victim to cognitive biases and trying to make patterns out of coincidences. Haumea was a small place; she should see the same people over and over, and for the most part, she did. The same barista made the coffee every morning, and the same janitors swept and dusted around the port offices at night. She categorized the guy as obviously unaware of her and, therefore, could be set aside for later analysis.

The end of the corridor had two doors; one turned 90 degrees to her left, and the other opened straight on into the hangar. She intended to pause momentarily before going through it, but the door opened on her approach. She immediately felt her senses sharpen and her focus return. These weren't the kind of doors that automatically opened for anyone, which meant that someone had been watching her approach and had opened the door for her. She resisted the urge to put her hand on her gun, kept herself upright, and walked purposefully into the hangar. What she saw was completely unexpected.

Watt had spent days pouring over the records of Haumea. Transactional receipts, ship registrations, and bookkeeping entries of dozens of companies could all be used as paper trail camouflage to hide illicit business or criminal activity from an investigator like Watt. Watt was good at her job, and she had been putting a lot of effort into finding a needle in the haystack of Haumea. Walking into that hangar and seeing that ship was like finding out that there had been a rhinoceros in the haystack the whole time, and she'd missed it every day. She stopped walking and stood for a minute. It was impossible. A ship this big couldn't be missed on the registries. A ship this big would have to leave a paper trail a mile wide. She'd even scoured the planetary radars and cross-checked them against hangar openings and closings to see if people were trying to hide multiple ship movements under single reports. How could she have missed *this*?

Astonished, she stood staring at the ship. How did this ship completely avoid her detection? More importantly, what exactly was this ship? It was clearly not a freighter or a private yacht, and she'd never seen a navy ship like this, although maybe it was some experimental spy ship that didn't get a lot of exposure landside. 'Was this even a ship?' she thought.

She couldn't even tell which direction was forward; it had no visible thrusters or engines. As she swept her eyes back and forth across the hull, movement drew her gaze. Two square meters of the smooth metal fractured into a spiderweb of geometric shapes. The gaps between the shapes grew, and the shapes were free to rotate and move like perfect machine parts. The shapes between the fractures started to twirl into two spirals, each with two spiral arms like little metal galaxies. The spirals spun and turned around each other. The pieces that made up the spirals turned within their little galaxies. Without abruptness, the arms of the spirals began to straighten out, and the constituent geometric shapes that composed them were coalescing together. The arms of each galaxy finally stopped moving as straight vertical bars. The tiny geometric shapes were now gone, seamlessly making up these two flat vertical bars. The bars hovered centimeters away from the ship's side, an empty hole in the hull behind them that had contributed the metal to their formation. Their stillness was only momentary before they turned into a viscous liquid flowing down the surface of an unseen staircase, continuing until the stairs became visible and covered in the liquid metal.

"Please, won't you join me inside?" a pleasant voice from everywhere asked.

Watt thought for a moment. Should she pull out her gun? Should she run back the way she came? Should she demand that the owner of the voice meet her on her terms? She had faced arsonists, terrorists, murderers, and mobsters in her past, and there were times when it was downright frightening. It didn't take long for her to assess this as some sort of pre-meeting intimidation ritual to demonstrate technical superiority and to flaunt their ability to stay hidden.

'Well, if they were showing off, if they were posturing, it would be because they had something to lose,' she thought. She decided on a tactic: she would meet on their terms and learn as much as she could without committing to anything. She thought briefly that if she walked up the stairs as if nothing was out of the ordinary, it would read as her trying too hard to be nonchalant and betray her tactic. Instead, she decided to diminish the spectacle by poking around the metal stairs and couching it as just a *neat trick*. It was, after all, pretty impressive. She walked over to the stairs, and before she stepped up to the door, she bent forward and ran her finger along the edge of the metal. There wasn't an unseen staircase underneath the metal. It seemed now that the metal had just flowed into the shape of a staircase. It also looked as though the liquid metal staircase stopped a centimeter or so above the floor and was clearly not touching the ship's hull. It felt like a solid when she touched it with her fingers, and even though she couldn't see what was holding it up, it *was* undoubtedly being held up by something.

Watt stood, straightened herself, and promptly walked up the stairs into the hole in the ship's side.

After entering, she walked down a hall a few meters until it curved, and she came upon a cozy table and a comfortable-looking chair. Atop the table was a single mug, with some steam coming from what Watt assumed was either coffee or tea. Across from the empty chair and full mug sat a man with perfectly black shiny skin and impossibly long fingers with too many joints. The man was wearing what appeared to be a bathrobe.

"Please, have a seat. There's no reason for alarm," Ymir said. "I'm sure I'm not what you were expecting, so let me introduce myself. My name is Ymir."

Watt stayed quiet as she took the seat. She kept her hands in her lap, indicating she was not gullible enough to drink from the suspect mug.

"Very well, I know you're a busy person. I've asked you here to make a request of you," Ymir said.

He paused for the slightest moment and smiled to himself before continuing. "I'm sure you've found yourself across the table from many unscrupulous characters in your days, listening patiently to them offering you bribes or threats, one way or another asking you to stop investigating because they know you're a bloodhound and they're at the end of the scent trail. I can see that, too. I'm at the end of your trail, and you don't even know who I am yet. Well, allow me to shine a flashlight down that trail for you and tell you what you'll find."

Ymir reached out, took the unwanted coffee mug into his monstrous hands, and took a sip before continuing his speech, this time with a bedtime story tone.

"You would eventually find my ship. My 'fog of mystery' can only hide it for so long. When you do, you'll investigate to see if I have some connections with the bombings. You'll clearly distrust any paperwork evidence out of a reasonable assumption that I've altered it, so you'll use up some shoe leather and start talking to your local contacts again. This time, with specific pressure. They'll know you're onto them and they might give you something. Especially a rat named Moet. He'll tell you three lies: First, that he has no culpability. This is obvious because he's just trying to stay out of trouble. Second, he'll tell you that I'm the guy you're looking for. He doesn't have any evidence for this, but he figures that any patsy you bust is better than attention turned his way. Third, he'll lie about the pile of money I gave him and what he used it for."

Watt made a mental note to herself to break one of Moet's fingers the next time they talked. She didn't say a word but kept eye contact to encourage Ymir to keep babbling. When guilty people ramble, they often self-incriminate.

"Well, you'd know Moet is lying to you about something. So, you'd double-check his story. When you do, you'll find out he's been chirping with the CGI through some pretty deep back channels. I imagine you've got CGI contacts, perhaps even friends there. They will warn you to stay away from this, and then they'll do what they think is right and report it up the channels. A few short days later, the Navy is here," Ymir said, then stopped talking.

"Are you trying to intimidate me with the Navy showing up? I think that's bad for you, not bad for me. You've got to work on better threats, friend," Watt said, cooly.

"I'm not threatening you. I'm asking for your help with something. I'm not expecting you'll change any of this part of the story. I'm just telling you what's going to happen as a courtesy," Ymir said.

"So, what is it that you want me to help you with, Mr. Ymir? You want me to conveniently look the other way about your involvement in some investigation, I suppose," Watt asked directly. She didn't want to give any information about what she was investigating, so she made a conscious effort to omit details.

Ymir smiled. It made Watt's skin crawl.

"Nothing of the sort. I actually want you to blame me for something." Ymir tried to look friendly but unfortunately came off as fiendish. He saw the minute signs of unease in Watt's expression and increased the concentration of aerosol endocrine signaling molecules to ensure her comfort and compliance. After a moment, her face visibly eased, and she seemed much more receptive to whatever he was going to say.

Twenty minutes later, Watt was walking away from the hangar, her mind racing and her feet drumming autonomously underneath her. She was too busy thinking to think about where she was going. The narrow corridor gave way to the tall ceilings of the crowded market hall, but even the noise and bustling passersby didn't break through her impenetrable shell of concentration.

CHAPTER SIXTEEN

Investigator Watt and Investigator Eiteng stood shoulder to shoulder, looking at a live image on a screen showing a small room with three chairs against the wall. In one of those chairs sat Ray Sanbadar, his hands handcuffed in his lap.

"Remarkable, how did you find him?" Eiteng asked.

"ACI brought me in to find out who was behind a few local bombings - nothing big. I stumbled across a few anomalies that ultimately led me to him," Watt responded. While she was averse to outright lying, she was okay with selectively omitting facts, leaving Eiting with a view of the situation that could generously be described as 'oversimplified.'

"Who was doing the bombings?" Eiteng asked.

"A local nobody who wanted to make a name for himself. He had found some connections with a corrupt vice chancellor in the GCI. The vice chancellor was manufacturing reasons for the GCI to take over Haumea so it could be annexed into his prefecture and presumably make him incredibly wealthy. But it turns out they're growing out of the crime game here. If it were fifty years ago, he probably would've been able to carve himself a good slice of the pie. It's all in my report. I suspect you'll want to put someone on him to see if he has conspirators before you make your recommendations for arrest, but taking down chancellors is well above my pay grade," Watt said.

"Yeah, I will, and I will review the situation. It's too easy for people to become corrupt this far out," Eiteng sighed.

Watt tried to ensure he didn't see her rolling her eyes.

"The local constabulary was more than adequate to apprehend the parties responsible for the destruction of the Leopard and Mr. Sanbadar. Councilwoman Poggs committed her enthusiastic support in the API investigation as well as valuable assistance in the Naval matter. I think they're starting to do alright out there in their little spaceport in the dark," Watt hinted at a gentle rebuff of Eiteng's assertion of corruption.

They both were right in a sense. Poggs got to where she was through corruption and no small amount of violence. Still, she seemed to be outgrowing that and earnestly developing Haumea into a stable and independent protectorate.

"Well, they didn't seem to do much to capture the Navy's fugitive. Although neither did the Navy so I hardly think they're to blame for that. As for this one, I see no sense in keeping him locked up like this. It's a long ride to Saturn, and I'd rather present him to the Navy as having been rescued by ACI rather than being imprisoned. Is that in keeping with your assessment of the situation? Or do you estimate that the Navy will view him as a criminal and that we will look foolish having let him roam around the ship?" Eiteng asked.

"Sanbadar was a confederate of the fugitive in the past, but I believe that confidence was broken, and he was taken as a hostage. He might not have been fully aware of his status as a hostage, as the fugitive is clearly persuasive and capable of planning elaborate ruses. I believe he is harmless, but it is probably prudent to continue to handle him with some measure of caution. I advise a modified custody arrangement for the duration of the flight: confinement to private quarters during curfew hours, as well as mandatory supervision by authorized personnel during the day. We don't need to be explicit about his conditions of restriction being unique to him, he might just figure that it is standard procedure for guest quarter doors to be locked, but I think we should make a show of unshackling him and giving him the impression of release. That way we won't get complaints from him if the Navy wanted him treated as a guest, but if they wanted him treated as a prisoner, we can credibly say that he was under confinement at all times." Watt laid out her plan.

It was a typically rational and well-reasoned

argument, precisely as Eiteng had come to expect from her. His slightest smirk went unnoticed by Watt. He recognized another attribute of her plan that was common enough not to be mistaken for a coincidence; even though her plan was logically framed, compassion had a place. Eiteng took a moment to appreciate how skillful Watt was to make it effortless for him to make a compassionate choice. He was proud of every aspect of her performance as an investigator, and it was exactly this kind of choice that gave him peace of mind regarding his upcoming retirement. He hadn't told Watt he planned on announcing her as his successor. He wondered if she had an inkling about it. She certainly didn't behave like she was vying for a promotion, but he doubted that he could surprise her with any announcement that big.

"That sounds like a good plan. I'll leave it to you," Eiteng said to Watt.

* * *

The door to the room where Ray was being held slid open. Watt's silhouette in the doorway wasn't the imposing figure Ray expected. She walked over to him and gestured that he should raise his hands. She grasped the metal cuffs in her right hand and placed her left wrist across the sensor strip on the top of the right cuff. The proximity of her watch band, combined with verbal authorization, unlocked the handcuffs. In situations with more dangerous prisoners, additional levels of security would have been used. However, with someone like Ray, the handcuffs were mostly just a visual reminder of who was in custody.

"Care for a cup of coffee? I know a great place just around the corner," Watt finally spoke.

"I thought we were in a ship," Ray said, rubbing his wrists awkwardly. Watt dropped her attempt at being charming and looked at him like he was a moron.

"Yes, Mr. Sanbadar, we are. This ship is equipped with a coffee machine." She tried not to sound sarcastic and insulting, a struggle to be sure. Ray looked embarrassed. She knew he had more or less been kidnapped by Pogg's goons and was just asking what was going on. It was unfair of her to judge him as dumb for asking that.

"I'll explain everything. I promise," Watt said, turning the charm back on.

The two walked into the adjacent room, clearly a breakroom and recreation area for a ship's crew. A square table stood in the center, and a coffee machine graced the countertop on the side of the room as in every breakroom in the fleet. If a crew were lucky, a break room would be large enough for a couch, usually far past its prime. The upright and businesslike chairs were the kind companies buy for employees to sit in. They were clearly made for planet-side use and had been retrofitted to index into notches in the floor for 0g use. Since they were walking in what felt to Ray like about .3g, he correctly surmised that the ship was still accelerating. The chairs pulled free of their indexing grooves, and the pair sat comfortably. Ray leaned back, a feat that he was much better at in reduced gravity than full Earth gravity. He always felt too close to falling over whenever he was in 1g or above.

"So, I suppose you have questions," Watt said into her coffee.

"Not as many as you'd think. I'd just like to be assured that you're going to treat Ymir well," Ray said. He sounded resigned.

Watt realized what kind of assumptions he must have made about what happened.

"Oh, I'm sorry to have let you think something bad happened to your friend. He wasn't apprehended on Haumea; only you were."

Ray didn't respond, pondering his words, clearly not in a talkative mood. She watched the look on his face change from confusion to satisfaction. She could almost hear him think through this new piece of information. Almost hear him question how it was possible he had been found, but Ymir had remained hidden. The teary smile on his face revealed so much. It told her that Ray was happy to have underestimated his friend and that he didn't know if he had escaped through some improvisational trickery or through some cunning and thorough preordained plan. She could tell it didn't matter because he knew his friend was still free.

Ray collected himself from his thoughts, and the smile disappeared. There was a long moment. Neither of them spoke. They sat in silence, sharing the feeling that silence was what was right because the actions that mattered were out of their control. Together, they took ownership of the quiet.

Watt felt crushed by a leaden blanket of

heartbreak at what she was about to tell Ray. She knew it was only a matter of time before their situation would be changed, either because they were found and caught, or they found what they were looking for. Ymir chose to never see his friend again. He didn't ask him, and he didn't even tell him that the choice had been made.

Watt understood that Ymir had recruited her to give credibility to the narrative that Ray wasn't culpable for helping Ymir escape or, at the very least, was an unwitting hostage. Ymir was protecting his friend by betraying him. He would take on the blame and guilt of a kidnapping - one that had never occurred - only to make his friend seem more innocent when the time came that they would finally have to split.

Watt knew she was the linchpin that would make that narrative hold. Ray could screw it up royally if he were foolish enough to convince the Navy that Ymir hadn't kidnapped him. He hadn't, of course, and Watt sensed that Ray would go to just as great lengths to protect Ymir. Her stomach sank. If Ray said the wrong things when the Navy debriefed him, he could be court martialed for treason. At the very least, Watt would lose her job and probably face charges of criminal conspiracy for her filing of false reports. She couldn't let Ray remain ignorant. She needed time.

"I'll show you to your quarters." She stood abruptly and adopted an unmistakably professional tone to her voice. His room was small but comfortable. She gave a brief tour of the amenities and communication panel. She bid him a comfortable stay and good rest before leaving him locked in his room. He sat on the bed. Exhaustion crashed down on him.

Sometime later, the lights in the room came on, waking Ray. He hadn't realized that he had fallen asleep. The door opened, and Watt walked directly through the room into the bathroom. She immediately retreated to the doorway to the main room. Ray thought it was an odd thing to do. She made brief eye contact with Ray and then looked back at the bathroom. She kept looking into the darkened bathroom while she spoke.

"Just checking in to make sure everything is in order." Her tone was curiously flat. She left the lights on, turned on her heel, and left the room. The door closed behind her. Ray squeezed his eyes tightly and swung his feet down to the floor. He wondered if she always acted this strangely. He thought momentarily and decided that she hadn't been checking to make sure things were in order. She must have been looking for something specific. He stood and went to the door. It stayed shut when he approached. There was no manual handle, and the rectangular control panel next to the door showed a simplified icon of a human stepping through a doorway with a large circle and a slash through it. It was clear, and frankly unsurprising, that he was locked in. So, what was she looking for in the bathroom? He patted his hand along the wall in the darkened bathroom, looking for something to turn on the lights with. He then looked up at the darkened ceiling and spoke to no one in particular.

"Hi. Um. Can the lights be on in here, please?" He felt kind of silly trying voice activation without knowing if that's how this ship worked. Sure enough, the lights faded on pleasantly, and he could suddenly see his surroundings. He was facing the mirror, with the sink to his left. There was a small shower stall and a toilet behind him. Pretty standard fittings for a ship. On the small countertop in front of him was a piece of paper. He picked it up and examined it. It was a handwritten note that read:

I've been in contact with your friend. He said he has a plan and that it requires the GCI to be convinced that you were kidnapped. Destroy this note. We are <u>never</u> to speak of this.

Ray tossed the note into the incinerator toilet and burned it. He shut the lights off and returned to bed. He was asleep as soon as he hit the pillow.

* * *

Watt sat at a small workstation in the back of the bridge. She tried not to lean against anything important on the console. Looking into her mug, she was in a mood to enjoy a cup of coffee but didn't want to actually drink any of it. Especially not this stuff; it seemed about as enjoyable as most ships' coffee.

She felt uncomfortable about Ray's situation. She hadn't exactly lied to him, but he certainly didn't have a complete and honest picture of what had happened. But in her own defense, Ray wasn't even her problem, and he probably didn't even know about the Leopard. On the other hand, his friend had dropped a trove of incriminating evidence in her lap about the vice chancellor's corruption, so doing right by Ray seemed justifiable. She brought the mug closer to her lips, paused, and then set it down again. One good turn deserves another, right?

CHAPTER SEVENTEEN

Colvard went weightless in her seat for the first time in almost three weeks. The feeling was incredible, like taking off boots laced too lightly for a very long day. The Fuego had been burning for eighteen days, the longest she had ever accelerated for. Living for almost six weeks at 1.6 times normal gravity was tough on anyone. The first day in high G acceleration is tiring but nothing like the next few. Waking up the first few days is like living a nightmare where you are still tired from the workout of your life, and it just won't ever end. You want to drink a cup of coffee, but you're not sure you want to spend the energy to hold your arms up to do it. Colvard had done plenty of high G burns and knew she would be asked to do plenty more. She chuckled a bit at the thought that even way out in weightless space, soldiers still had to carry heavy loads. She guessed it was some immutable law of the universe.

Colvard's law: For every soldier, there is an equal and opposite really heavy thing to carry around. She committed to work on the wording a bit, but she liked the sound of it.

She moved the muscles of her face around. She felt effervescent from the relief of the weight. She floated gently against her seat restraints but could barely feel it. Her tongue felt like it was swelling in her mouth. She took a moment to tie her hair back better and then looked down at the console to check their route. The Fuego was now moving at eight percent of the speed of light. At this very moment, Colvard was pretty sure that they were the farthest ship away from the sun. It made her feel pretty lonely for a second. They burned through a ton of fuel to make it out this far in such a hurry. A Dart can usually operate for several years before needing a refuel, depending on the specific mission profile. The Fuego would have to take it slow on the burn back to Saturn.

The pleasant weightlessness would only last a few minutes before Colvard would turn the Fuego around and begin their deceleration. Leftenant Armister floated out of his seat and groaned in relief. He pretended to be unaware of where he was floating when he bumped his posterior into the back of Colvard's head.

"You best stow that thing, sonny. We're too far out for a resupply of my patience." Colvard had the slightest sing-song tone that let her shipmate know she was having fun but was still at the limits of her tolerance. The oversized and out-of-place leftenant feigned ignorance about his transgression. Smirks were surreptitiously exchanged around the ship.

"Aaaaaand it's stowed," Armister said, his voice trailing off as he floated toward the rear of the ship.

"Fastest man in the system, and still, you're that slow," a voice from the comms station threw out a quip. Colvard wouldn't reprimand the informality, nor would she engage in it. In GCI advanced leadership training, Colvard wrote her term paper on the paradox of leniency promoting discipline. It seemed so much easier for her to find examples from naval history of times when commanders allowed their crews to break the rules so that they would be more reliably obedient in the future than it was to induce the same behavior in her own crew. She felt like she was simultaneously betraying the order and structure of the Navy by allowing meaningless transgressions and being a distant and detached leader to her crew by not acknowledging the human aspect of living in close quarters with the same people for months at a time. Long ago, she imagined that leading a crew would be like finding the footpath that walks along the ridge of a mountain range, stepping too far to one side or the other, and you'll have plenty of time to think about your mistakes as you tumble down the mountainside. But now it seemed like she was somehow falling down both sides of the mountain simultaneously, like there was no path on the top for her to walk. She thought about being stricter, but that seemed worse. Then she thought about being more lenient, and that also seemed worse. Maybe she was tumbling down two mountains simultaneously, but at least she was trying to tumble as slowly as possible. She chuckled to herself at how low she was setting the bar for herself, then she quickly stifled her chuckling so that no one would notice.

"We've got forty-one minutes until we initiate decel. Enjoy the tau because you'll be a few hours younger than the desk jockeys back at SatSys."

Colvard settled on this declaration as a good balance between re-establishing mission priority and allowing a bit of time to goof around. The forty-one minutes were planned into the route from the beginning, but that didn't keep her from treating it as a concession that she gave by her grace. She wanted to talk with someone more about the relativistic shift in time that they were experiencing and how they would return to the Saturnian System having fewer hours pass aboard their ship than what passed on the stations. Sure, it was only a few hours, but Colvard was excited and proud that they had done this. This mission was a rarity. Most crews would fly for a whole career and never get near this speed. There were crews that had been faster in the past. For a few days, they were the fastest humans in the entire solar system, which was one fact that would surely come up after a few drinks for years and years to come.

* * *

Under the surface ice of IP10-06 and almost seven kilometers of water, an enormous machine lumbered over smooth boulders. A five-meter wide comb-toothed scoop dragged through the regolith on the ocean floor in front of the three-meter tall wheels.

The comb teeth jiggled and bounced the rocks and debris about, shaking some into the storage bin and most of it out the bottom back onto the surface. It looked chaotic, but the machine was good at its task. It discarded pieces high in silicone or aluminum and selected pieces with substantial amounts of heavier elements and more useful metals.

The big machine bathed the planet's surface in front of it with high-energy X-rays and looked for the characteristic patterns of elements in the backscatter of the radiation. Rocks with a bit extra bismuth reflected just so, whereas rocks with a high amount of uranium ore had their own peculiar X-ray luster. This X-ray energy also scrambled every microbial cell on those rocks. The biofilms that clung to the surface of the boulders and rocks were either completely disaggregated from a cell wall fracture or were irreparably scrambled internally from the excess of ionizing radiation. Only the rare one in a billion cells survived the astronomically high X-ray blast, and only one in a billion of those would live long enough to successfully reproduce, but even under the blast of radiation from the alien machine, life wasn't going to give up.

The radiation from the X-ray sweep was negligible compared to the deadly flood of alpha and beta particles coming from the machine's unshielded reactor. The air around the five metal columns hummed and crackled with life and glowed faintly with Cherenkov radiation. It was alive. Alive with a kind of life that was poison to all other life. Alive with radiation.

The machine picked up a surprising and extraordinary rock. It was entirely metal, heavier than aluminum. This rock had more metal in it than the sum of the collection from the entire morning and mostly heavy, valuable metals. Within moments, the machine had scanned and analyzed the metal to 99.9% confidence of being an asteroid. The roving machine felt no excitement; it was incapable. After several more hours of scanning back and forth, scouring the cold planet for metals, the machine was back at its station to offload and recharge. The collected rocks were sifted and sorted into a hopper that fed into a smelting forge. The smelter was typical of what would be found in an early colonizing setup. It had a ceramic centrifuge that could separate metals by their density. It was terribly inefficient, but it could turn rocks into usable extruded metal bars.

The metal bars were banded and stacked neatly on a flattened portion of the seafloor near the forge. A series of squat, squarish robots took the bars, stack by stack, across the sea floor to a lattice tower a kilometer and a half from the forge. The lattice tower was a circular column 150 meters in diameter, constructed entirely of the bars from the forge welded into a tessellating pattern of triangles. A ring of six pylons anchored the tower into the rock bottom, and the column formed graceful arches between pylons. The squat, squarish robots carried their bundles through these arches into the center of the column where the lattice had six hollow inner columns; half were used for robots going up, the other half for robots going down. The arrangement appeared like a geometrically perfect aerenchyma of an enormous metal plant stem. The squat robots attached themselves to parallel metal rails and began hoisting their bundles of metal upward.

As they climbed, the robots passed rings of thirty-two tanks of air harvested as a byproduct of the forging process. The tanks, located at each 150 m level, were sized and pressured appropriately to provide as much buoyancy as the 150 meters of metal bars beneath them. Once completed, the lattice would have forty-five rings of tanks, 1440 in total, holding its entire weight. The completed lattice would be tolerant to failures of individual tanks and lattice bars, and very close to neutrally buoyant. Every 450 meters, a trio of guy wires extended down to the seafloor to stabilize the lattice against ocean currents. The location chosen for the lattice was the primary protection against the lateral forces of the ocean currents. IP10-06 spun on its axis like any other planet.

The Coriolis effect arranged the ocean currents into circumferential bands with upwelling and downwelling zones between them. In certain places around the planet, such as those narrow upwelling and downwelling zones, there was very little lateral current flow in the middle depths of the water column where the lattice would be most vulnerable to shear forces. This lattice was built in an upwelling zone, so for most of the climb up the hollow inner columns, the water current rose with the robots, assisting in lifting their heavy bundles of metal. The lifting robots were also assisted with a pair of ballast tanks filled with oxygen, a byproduct of the smelting of aluminum. The empty robots returning to the seafloor would fill their ballast tanks with water and simply sink along the parallel rails until they reached the bottom.

Building the lattice in an upwelling zone was also ideal for the conditions at the surface. The top of the lattice couldn't be attached to the ice because the ice flow would simply carry away anything that was attached to it. The upwelling zone was where two ice sheets were pushed apart, making a much easier job of maintaining open seawater above the lattice. The comparatively warm ocean water loaded the cold atmosphere with water vapor that would cycle up through the clouds and flutter back down onto the massive ice flows, adding layer by layer every day. The endless currents ringing the planet would drive the ice flows against each other, crushing the massive sheets into smaller and smaller bits that would melt faster because of their increased surface area. The planet had been repeating this same pattern for millions of years. The only variation was from the frequent seafloor volcanoes or very infrequent sizeable meteor impacts.

The surface structure of this lattice was still under construction. It was formed by ninety-one hexagonal hulls floating on the surface, linked by their edges. Each hexagon was nine meters on an edge, so the entire platform of hexagons covered the top of the lattice with a few meters overhang. The hexagons tessellated together to create a relatively large surface but still had the flexibility to move with any waves. The ice flows dampened most of the wave activity on IP10-06, and since there was no moon or sun, there were no tides, so the ocean's depth stayed relatively consistent.

On the surface, a team of robots methodically navigated through the slow-motion storm of ice flows. The ice sheets on IP10-06 could be dozens or hundreds of square kilometers but rarely ever reached more than a few dozen meters thick. The largest ice flows found a balance between two currents, spun by opposite pulls on either end. These massive ice flows would create enormous ice circles, hewn almost perfectly round by their perpetual spinning. Like the giant red eye of Jupiter, giant ice circles on IP10-06 would dominate the planet's surface if the faint starlight was enough to light it up. Also, like the red eye of Jupiter, the giant ice circles would only last a few thousand years before wobbling too far into one current and ultimately breaking apart into smaller pieces.

Tracked robots dragged cables over the surface of one of the wider ice flows on an errant path directly toward the surface site of the lattice. Buoyant robots crawled upside down along the underside of the ice flow, pulling the other end of the cables. A series of holes had been drilled along estimated fracture lines, and metal rods inserted. When heated, the metal rods would melt some of the ice, filling the drill holes with warm water. This warm water would slowly warm the ice around it, causing expansion and fractures deep within the ice. The cables would be stretched around the fracture lines and pulled taut. The immense pressure of the cables would guide the growing cracks in the ice. Once the cracks were seeded and growing, massive subsonic drivers would be actuated, and their heavy vibrations would shake the ice flow apart. By forcing the two halves of the ice flow apart, the gap between them could be widened so that each side slid past the surface structure of the lattice without endangering it.

If a large enough iceberg threatened the web of floating hexagons, they could be detached, moved around the iceberg, and reassembled back in place once it had passed. If a passing iceberg couldn't be moved out of the way and the depth was great enough to impact the lattice, the top section of the lattice would be severed and floated away to avoid damage to the rest of the column.

In a single-story structure on one of the hexagonal tesserae sat Ygir, his face lit by three screens. Ygir kept a close watch on the information on the screen. It didn't change. Thirty-one hundred kilometers away, a dirigible floated three hundred meters above the ocean's surface. The dirigible was one of countless hydrogen-filled ovoids loitering around the surface of the planet. Ygir had yet to develop an industrial-scale space launch facility, so his space assets were limited to a few dozen probes and satellites already aboard the freighter in orbit. The dirigibles were autonomous and buoyed in the heavy atmosphere by a giant ovoid bladder filled with hydrogen derived from seawater. The particular dirigible of interest to Ygir was collecting data on the massive magnetic field generated by the pattern of coils laying on the seafloor so deep beneath it. The dirigible was recording its information to be relayed later to an identical sistership station ninety-eight km away. The sistership had moved to avoid a storm cell and was forced to move beyond the horizon into radio shadow. It would be several hours before it could attain an altitude high enough to reestablish communications. Once communications were restored to the first sistership, they would be relayed to a further chain of dirigibles that would carry along the data all the way back to Ygir. As it was, he sat frustrated, waiting for an update.

The update that Ygir was waiting on would eventually arrive, and he would be told that the gigantic electromagnetic coils laid out in kilometers-wide arcs across the seafloor were operating within expected parameters. The coils were laid out over what Ygir had surveyed to be a particularly active and hot vortex in the planet's mantle. This vortex of molten iron had carried heat from the planet's core up to the surface faster than in the surrounding areas. This extra heat had thinned out the planetary crust above the vortex.

The magnetic fields from Ygir's giant seafloor coils were designed to coax a bit more velocity out of the eddy of molten iron. The fields would pull at the magma, fluctuating and flowing as needed to accelerate the churning of heat from deep in the planet's core up to the surface. Enough heat to create a massive volcano that would blast rock and iron into the cold ocean year after year until it reached the sea's surface. Then, for the first time in almost a hundred million years, IP10-06 would have an island of dry land. It would be the first island in an archipelago to mark the ocean world with lifeless black rock. Ygir imagined what his islands would look like rising out of the ocean, lit by the dim stars. In a world where even the bright white ice was barely visible, the mountains would be like jagged voids in the clouds. Ygir closed his eyes and imagined the sound of ice being dragged against the windward side of the island. He imagined the black water on the leeward side, a channel free of ice for kilometers.

The set of coils that Ygir watched on his monitor was the first full-scale coils brought up to power. Crawling robots would drag dozens more into place in the coming months, and they would all be connected to function as one extensive network. Ygir's machines were creating coils fast enough that in only twenty-three days he could have a full coil network activated at full power.

After 750 Earth days of operation at full capacity, the coils would be recovered by seafloor crawlers and moved a safe distance away from the volcano site. The crust would be drilled, and a pattern of fusion bombs would be placed at strategic depths. The bombs would be detonated in a precisely timed pattern, with the outermost ring firing first. As the shockwave would expand towards the center, each successive ring would fire, adding power to the shockwave. Once the wavefront reached the center, its destructive power would be orders of magnitude beyond any single bomb. The concentrated shock wave would be directed directly up and directly down. The seismic energy directed downward would fracture and weaken the crust, accelerating the creation of the volcano. The energy directed upward would create a superheated fountain of steam that would be compressed back into liquid at the deepest depths.

Closer to the surface, the water would spontaneously boil and bubble tumultuously for days. The shockwave would create a moderate tsunami that would be detectable even after circling the planet several times but wouldn't pose any threat to Ygir's structures because the kilometers-deep ocean would allow the waveform to be extremely long and low. Even 3100 kilometers away, the ocean surface would rise four meters at the station where Ygir sat. He would make sure to be safely aboard a dirigible during that event.

CHAPTER EIGHTEEN

The Bonaparte's mess deck was 150 square meters and had seating for 120. None of the crew considered it cramped anymore. It was the largest space available to them that didn't require an EV suit. Thirty tables sat in six perfectly measured rows of five tables each. Each table had four immovable round stools that allowed the occupants to rest for their all too brief mealtimes. Two men in EV undersuits sat at one of the tables.

"You know who Martin reminds me of? That supply clerk at port. I wonder if they're related," Hollis said, mostly to his spoon.

"Which one?" Pierre asked.

"Which port?" Hollis looked confused.

"Which *Martin*?" Pierre said.

"Oh. Martin Christian, the one that looks like the clerk. Come on. What do you think? I was talking about Martin Sanders?"

"I think they're siblings," Pierre said.

"They never seem to hang out or talk to each other."

"Some siblings are that way. Maybe they don't like each other. You know, families."

"Hey. You know what Saiti told me? She said that we were going out to fight another cognate," Hollis said.

"Cognition," Pierre corrected.

"Whatever. Those things creep me out."

"You've never even seen one, I bet."

"No, but they're still creepy. I bet you haven't seen one, either," Hollis said.

"Nope," Pierre said.

The two men chewed their food in silence for a moment. Hollis took another scoop from the rapidly diminishing rectangular foodstuff in front of him and, with a flip of his spoon, tossed it into his mouth. His throw was low, but a lightning-fast duck saved the food from spatting onto his undersuit.

"I'm telling you..." Hollis said through a mouth full of food, "this is way more than 0.2g acceleration. We're really burning fast to get out there."

"Well, that's how the Admiral does it. Those planets out there aren't going to blow themselves up," Pierre said.

"Did I ever tell you that my dad was in the fleet with him when he took out Mars?"

"No, you didn't. I was on the ship with him when he did it, too," Pierre said as he wiped his chin. "What did your dad do?"

"Holy shit! You never told me that. You were there!

Like front and center there? What was it like?" Hollis was tickled with excitement.

"It was the same as the toolroom always was. I was an enlisted machinist at that point. You've got to remember that was decades ago. I'd never met the Admiral at that point, I just knew he was the guy in charge," Pierre said nonchalantly.

After a few moments to recall, he went on, "In the toolroom, we didn't really have anything to do at first. It was exciting to hear the boomers going off. It really felt powerful. It got boring after a while, honestly. The whole first day, we really just sat there and waited for something to break, but nothing happened. Sixteen-hour shifts during engagements, by the way. Old school. Well, on day-two, stuff started breaking, and it just didn't stop. There's no machine that can take that much energy for that long, the guns were just smashing themselves apart. By the end of it, we had broken just about everything on the ship. It was a lot of work."

"I wonder what it would do if we let loose on one of the gas giants. Ever think about that?" Hollis asked.

"No, I hadn't, but I can't imagine we would do much. We certainly couldn't destroy them." Pierre twisted his eyebrows unconsciously with the effort of thought.

"I mean, if we hit the core," Hollis said.

"I don't know if we could ever get it to fracture; the thing is so dense. And any fragmentation certainly wouldn't leave the atmosphere. But I suppose it would stir it up a bit. I bet we'd stir up a bunch of new vortices between atmospheric layers, which would throw off a few planet-sized storms, but other than that, not much."

"Not much? Planet-sized storms?" Hollis asked incredulously.

"Guess you've got a point. For a planet that's mostly gas, I guess wind is a pretty big deal," Pierre said.

"Well, it's not like anyone's living on Jupiter anyway. If he's going to blow up anything, it'll be a moon."

"He's not going to blow anything up."

"You mean *other* than Ceres?" Hollis jibed. Pierre clucked his teeth and nodded in agreement.

"Yeah, I guess that was pretty crazy. It still seems sort of surreal. I mean, one guy fighting the whole damn fleet and getting in some damn good hits. I mean, we lost the Boston and the Shannon, for Chrissake. Those ships were bloody invincible," Pierre said, shaking his head.

"That's why the Admiral's going to smite him next time. Wherever he is, he can't hide," Hollis declared.

"Well, if the Admiral blows up too many more places, we won't have anywhere left to dock."

"I'm telling you, Pierre, the Admiral is out for blood," Hollis said.

CHAPTER NINETEEN

The blood dripped into the sink. Agrablatt swore under his breath and gently touched the wound on his chin. He bent to rinse the blood from the gash and then leaned in close to the mirror for a good look. On the sink in the tiny bathroom sat an ancient block of soap that had miraculously stayed the same size for years, despite sloughing and oozing a thick layer of soap scum into the basin. The soap had sat so long that it discolored the actual metal of the sink itself.

Haumea loved to display its grand halls, with all that open space and foot traffic, but most of the city was cramped spaces that felt like economy-class berths on a ship. Space is vast, but space on Haumea was limited, and therefore extremely expensive. Agrablatt lived where he worked, in Poggs's personally owned stoat kennels. The kennels were located in Agricultural Dome 3, a small region reserved for maintenance and utility work. Agrablatt liked the seclusion. It allowed him to go about his days, grumbling, the stoats his only audience, without any interference from other people.

Poggs had a talent for finding a place for everyone. Agrablatt had an inflexible personality, and even in his previous job as a janitor, he couldn't avoid friction with his employer. He had initially come to Haumea years earlier, as so many did, penniless and with only the clothes on his back. How he was able to afford the transit fare was anyone's guess. He claimed to be a mechanic but was a slow worker prone to outbursts of vitriol and profanity. He had issues holding any jobs he'd been hired for, often fired in the first few days. He was able to keep his job as a janitor for two years, primarily by avoiding contact with everyone else. Eventually, what little contact he made proved to be intolerably strident and crass, and he was let go again. He quickly ran out of money and was evicted. Poggs kept strict tabs on where people were living in her city, requiring all landlords and homeowners to submit reports of changes in housing status. Her system identified that Agrablatt was reported as being evicted from his very cheap apartment and had no corresponding applications to another apartment. Within hours of becoming homeless, he was picked up by Poggs's men and brought in. He had a brief interview with a clerk who took detailed notes, and then he was brought to Poggs herself.

Agrablatt was escorted into Poggs's office by a large man whose evident occupation was to look intimidating. The stone-faced heavy pointed at the floor where Agrablatt was to stand. Agrablatt dutifully complied. Without speaking, the heavy's huge hand reached out and took off Agrablatt's hat and pushed it into his chest for him to hold. Agrablatt clutched the hat against his chest with both hands. The heavy silently stepped back and made a convincing impression of a statue.

"Seems yar a torn a man," Poggs said. Agrablatt didn't understand. He stood silently for a moment before turning to the heavy for a clue. The heavy continued to act out his role as a statue.

"Yar a torn in everyone's foot. No'hbody wan' it," Poggs repeated.

"Oh, a *thorn* in your foot. I don't mean to be a thorn in nobody's foot, ma'am," Agrablatt started but cut himself short when Poggs lifted a bony finger to silence him.

"No'h *mie* foot. Mie foot have no torns. Other people step on dem. No'h me. I know no'h ta step an dem. Ya know de bes' way for a torn?" Poggs paused long enough to let Agrablatt shake his head.

"'Tis on de bush... where tis useful... where tisn'h goin' ta get under mie foot," Poggs said, then pausing for a time. Agrablatt's knuckles hurt from squeezing his hat so tightly.

She continued, "Ih can'h make ya wha' ya're no'h... but Ih can putch ya war ya won'h be stept on."

Poggs leaned back in her chair and turned her attention to a file on her desk. The heavy's hand appeared on Agrablatt's shoulder, and he was led out of her office. She never spoke another word to him. The heavy indicated to Agrablatt to enter another door where the clerk from his earlier interview was waiting. The clerk explained with a lawyer-like formality that Chief Councilwoman Poggs was generously offering Agrablatt a job. Included with her offer was a relatively unique set of benefits and an equally unique set of stipulations. Specifically, he would be afforded free room and board as part of his pay. As part of his occupational obligations, he was expected to stay there and not cause any more problems. Agrablatt felt that accepting her offer was a far wiser choice than declining it. He signed some papers without reading them and was sent out of the building with only an address.

Upon arriving at the stoat kennels, Agrablatt was met by a teenage boy who greeted him with more professionalism and enthusiasm than he expected.

"Allo, sir. Ih assume ya're de new stoat keeper?" the boy said.

"Say what?" Agrablatt replied, obviously confused. The boy seemed to anticipate his confusion and rolled easily onward.

"Yes, sir. Ya're the new stoa' keeper. Righ' dis way, Ih'll show you aroun'," the boy said.

"What's a stoat?" Agrablatt asked, following behind the slim, young man clothed in a thick, tan canvas jumpsuit. He thought he caught a glimpse of a smirk on the boy's face as he turned around to walk towards the building. The agricultural domes all had massive light tubes for growing hydroponic vegetables. The brightness made Agrablatt's eyes ache. The agricultural dome was the largest area he had seen in years. Even the market halls made him a bit uncomfortable with how wide open they were. They just reminded him of his fear of the vacuum of space—not a deep, gripping fear, but an uneasy fear that made his spine feel itchy. The kennel building, however, was dim and cramped, and he felt much more comfortable inside.

"Dat be a stoat," the boy said, pointing to one of the many cages along a wall of cages. The cage was a metal box with a glass front. Inside it was a bowl of water and a blanket. On the blanket was a donut-shaped ring of fur. It took Agrablatt a moment to discern where the head and tail of the animal were, as it was so neatly coiled against itself. It lay motionless.

"What do I do with it?" Agrablatt asked plaintively.

"Ya keep it. Healty an' in good fightin' shape," the boy said.

"Oh, shit. These are those little things that they bet on? I've never seen one," Agrablatt said. He stood for a while, looking at the thing. "They're a lot smaller than I thought they'd be."

"500 grams. No'h a mote a dus' more, or dey aren'h allowed to figh'. No'h one wants ta pay far any a d'heavier weigh' class animals like badgers, at least no'h ou' har on Haumea, jus' too expensive. No'h when dese little guys grow so fas' an' figh' so har'."

"So, I'm supposed to grow them? I don't know anything about keeping pets," Agrablatt said, which made the boy laugh.

"Sir, dey no'h be pets. Um, ya bes' no'h tink dey be pets. Dey only live a few months at de mos', an' dey be really vicious. Ya definitely shouldn'h cuddle up wid one a dem."

"They sure don't look vicious," Agrablatt said.

"C'mon, Ih'll show ya wha' ta do," the boy said. He grabbed a metal box from the corner of the room and attached it to the front of the cage. "Dis be de transport cage. Ya can'h ever let them ou', or wey'll have ta kill dem. So, de're alway in one cage or 'nother. Ya can'h reach inta d'cages, or de'll rip ya ta shreds. R'ember, dese tings are genetihk-gineer'd to be fas' an' ferocious. So, look, ya click dese four latches, super importan', den ya slide dis an' den dat button will make de back wall a der cage push farward an' it pushes dem farward inta d'travel cage."

The wall slid forward hydraulically, pushing the dozing animal and its blanket toward the travel cage. When the wall tipped the bowl over, the animal woke up and hissed. Everything, including some of the animal's feces, was pushed unceremoniously into the travel cage. The boy slid another glass panel inta place an' latched it, then set the now-occupied box on the floor.

"Once d'wall cage is empty, ya can clean an' put new water in der. Puttin' dem back in der is sort a de reverse, but ya don't hafta push dem fra de travel cages. Dey usually go right inta d'wall cage, but if dey don'h, ya just hafta wait until dey get aroun' to it. Den, when de're locked in d'wall cage, ya can clean d'travel cage. An' it goes on like dat," the boy explained helpfully.

"Why do we have to kill them if they get out of the cage?" Agrablatt asked.

"Because ya couldn'h ever get dem back, an' de're too dangerous to be runnin' around. If one dem gets out d'cage when ya're in har, ya got ta put on dis oxygen mask an' pull dat yellow handle," the boy said pointing at a lever high up on the wall.

"Why is it all the way up there?" Agrablatt asked.

"Oh, ya're supposed ta be standin' on d'table. Dey can jump dat high, but when de're panicked, usually dey just run aroun' d'corners a d'room," the boy said.

"So, what does the handle do? Poison gas floods the room while I'm in it? Fuck that," Agrablatt said.

"Sorta. It be harmless ta us. Dey says it be a gas dat interacts only with dem because a de way de're engineered. Ih don'h know how it works, but dey says dat dey have special genes dat makes it so dey can be poisoned by the gas an' wey can'h. Ih don'h know why wey don'h get the special genes that make us no'h be poisoned. I also think it's kinda sketchy because dey give us d'mask an' everyting, so it can'h be completely safe."

"So, what happens after the thing dies?" Agrablatt asked.

"Oh, righ'. Jus' lif' d'lever back up ta d'normal position an' d'room will ventilate. D'doors will unlock once d'air be back ta normal."

"Fucking all of space," Agrablatt said to himself and shook his head. He looked exactly as grumpy as he usually did.

"So, dey eat dese." The boy pointed to a cage on the other wall filled with some other furry animal. "Ya have ta feed dem a certain times. D'book over der has d'schedule, but ya'll need ta figure it ou' ta each animal. Dat's kinda de tricky par'. Knowing how many days before d'fight ya can feed dem an' still have der weight down below 500g on d'day a d'fight. Dere's a scale over der. Put d'whole cage on it, den weigh it again once d'stoat is ou', an' ya can figure out how much it weighs. D'book also shows d'days dat ya need ta give d'different oils. D'bottles are in dat cabinet. Ya just pour it in der water bowl. Something about how dey grow, Ih don'h know wha' tis."

The boy opened the door of the food critters' cage, tilted it slightly, reached in, and grabbed one of the little animals. Agrablatt didn't recognize it, but it appeared to be some kind of rodent. The boy tossed the rodent into the empty wall cage, returned the loaded travel cage back up to the front, and latched it on. Agrablatt watched the rodent run frantically and helplessly against the back wall. The stoat clawed and gnashed at the glass panel. The boy glanced momentarily at Agrablatt before sliding out the glass panel that separated the two cages. The stoat was across the cage with the rodent in its mouth in the blink of an eye. Agrablatt expected more violence and thrashing, but it was so fast he hadn't even seen it move. It was just a blur for the briefest moment, and then it was still with its prey in its mouth.

Agrablatt spent the next three years as the stoat keeper. He wasn't exactly born for the job, but it was better than being a janitor. He liked being away from other people, but the stoats moved around and made just enough noise to fend off the lonely feeling of being in an empty room. He'd spend his days feeding the stoats and grumbling to himself about having to feed the stoats. Once a week, a short old man with a suspiciously full head of hair would come into the kennel and examine the stoats. He would silently stand in front of each cage and scribble notes about each animal. The first time he showed up and started taking notes, he didn't introduce himself and only rarely asked Agrablatt questions about the stoats.

Agrablatt didn't know for sure what the rest of that man's job entailed, but he assumed it had to do with coordinating the fights. When a fight was scheduled, the man would come in and select which stoats were to fight. Agrablatt would dutifully load them into travel cages and stack them on a cart, grumbling about it all the while.

Moet and Agrablatt would bring the stoats to the Colosseum, a bar adjacent to Hall A. The bar was cramped, maybe only 300 square meters of floor space, but having private space was a rarity on Haumea. When the Colosseum would host a fight, it would cram as many people as possible into the room, often well over a thousand spectators. The pair would show up early, and Moet would disappear into some backroom that Agrablatt had never seen. It was several months before Agrablatt learned that the man's name was Moet, and then it was only because he heard someone at a fight curse at him. He did enjoy grumbling at the occasional bar patron who got too close to the stoat cages, but the noise and the people irritated him, and he was always exhausted at the end of fight days.

* * *

The fights took place in custom glass containers with a door on either side that two stoat cages would be connected to. The doors would be opened, and the stoats would meet in the middle where the spectators could watch the carnage. As quickly as possible, the doors would be closed, and the cages removed so as not to impede anyone's view. The stoats never needed encouragement to fight; they were genetically-modified to be psychotically violent. Any animal that was in their sight was viciously attacked. Every fight resulted in death. Sometimes, the victorious stoat would only live a few minutes longer than its vanquished foe, but that was long enough for judges to declare which bettors were the winners.

Since all the animals were kept in the same kennel, the bettors could be reasonably well-assured that there wasn't any doping or cheating going on. Of course, there were always rumors that fights were fixed, primarily by people who lost a lot of money, but no one believed them. Betting on the fights was essentially a coin toss, only a very bloody one. Some people were happy to bet the minimum just to watch the fight, and if they won, it was just a bonus for them. Others cared more about the money on the line, carefully considered the fighters' attributes, and then applied their proprietary gamblers' logic to determine who the smart money would be on.

Chief Poggs kept strict rules that prohibited anyone involved in the administration of the fights from betting on only one contestant. She kept a loophole in the regulations, allowing the gift of a betting voucher to be exempt from taxes as a semi-official way to give bribes and payoffs to people she wanted to influence. She, or one of her subordinates, would bet substantial sums on both contestants and give the vouchers for the bets to whomever they were bribing. This had two effects: first, it made bribing people possible, albeit expensive, and second, it propped up the Colosseum financially.

The Colosseum was owned and operated by a man named Rivena Sterenca. Rivena's parents had grown up with Poggs on the rough streets of Humea and had been killed when the GCI opened fire on their ship as they tried to flee from a routine inspection. They had attempted to escape because aboard their freighter were several hundred kilos of drugs that they were smuggling on behalf of Poggs, who at the time had just started making a name for herself.

Poggs watched over Rivena from afar, making sure that he got the jobs he applied for, making sure that the gangs and bullies left him alone, and making sure that he wasn't exploited. Rivena didn't know any of this. In fact, when he applied to open the Colosseum, Poggs specifically made sure her covert support for him was hidden behind a thick screen of bureaucratic obstruction. He never spoke with her, knew her only by reputation, and had a vague disdain for her. She had quit the smuggling racket because of her remorse over his parents' death. She thought about him often and never got over the heartache she felt from orphaning him. He never knew any of it.

* * *

Agrablatt would never forget the first stoat fight he witnessed. It was seared into his memory. He had only been working with them for a few days. He thought he was familiar with the animals, but he was utterly unprepared for how fast and vicious they were. A sleek, sable male was pitted against a snow-white female. He assumed he'd be able to watch each move, each lunge, each dodge, but they were so fast and violent that he couldn't tell what was happening and then, within seconds, it was over.

It had been a ferocious spinning tangle of black and white fur that seemed to roll and shake in an entirely non-animalistic way. The amount of flesh and fur torn from each animal and the amount of blood left streaked and splattered around the inside of the glass cage made Agrablatt queasy. It was a terrifying fight to the death, performed in triple-time. Eyeballs and jawbones were torn off the animals and only recognizable once they settled unceremoniously on the cage floor. Stoats have a deep knowledge of how to kill, bestowed from generations of predatory ancestors. Evolution gave each stoat the urge to bite at the base of their opponent's skull; genetic engineering turned that urge into an uncontrollable fury. It was a horrific sight to watch.

On a day like any other, Agrablatt was working in the kennel when he heard movement on the other side of the door. Naturally, he expected Moet to come through the door and start to scribble his notes about the animals. The door to the kennel swung open as he expected, but against his expectations, it wasn't Moet who walked in but an elderly man.

"Beggin' yar pardon, sir, but Ih believe ya're goin' ta be late. An' ya don't want ta be late, sir," the old man said.

Agrablatt stood still, unsure if he'd ever seen this man before. He glared at him silently. Instead of asking any questions, Agrablatt stood like a glaring statue.

"Ih've been given instructions ta come find ya an' ta tell ya dat ya have important business ta attend. Ya're ta go ta d'Colosseum post haste, sir, an' wait dere far d'man named, er, Hamlet, sir," the elderly man explained.

"Hamlet?" grumbled Agrablatt. "What's this bloody all about? The Colosseum is clear on the other side of the station."

"Yessir, tis," the old man said. He followed it with a bit of a sigh and moved closer to Agrablatt to continue, "Ya do know, sir, who gives instructions? Don'h ya?"

Agrablatt thought to himself for a moment. He nodded and grumbled in acknowledgment.

The old man continued, "Wait a d'Colosseum. D'man named Hamlet will contact ya dere. Ya, erm, don'h wan' ta miss dis meetin' far anyting, sir."

Agrablatt grumbled, then trudged out the door. The elderly man followed him outside but then stopped just outside the open door. Agrablatt trudged down the path towards the tunnel between the agricultural dome and the main halls. It was a long walk. He stuffed his hands into his jacket pockets so he could grumble more effectively. As he got farther away from the kennel, the traffic thickened with more pedestrians and personnel carts. Not enough people to quite call it a crowd, but enough that he had to watch where he was going. Something in the back of his mind bothered him. Had the old coot left the kennel? Agrablatt turned around while walking, looking back toward the kennel. He was too far away to see it, but he thought looking in that direction would make everything make more sense. Looking back, he caught sight of Moet, facing rearward on a personnel cart. He looked uncomfortable. He was stuffed into the seat between two men, and it looked like he had a swollen lip.

"Eh, fuck it," Agrablatt grumbled to himself out loud. "If that crazy old man is going to screw with the stoats, Moet will walk in and catch him in the act. It's probably some gambling fix, that's why he sent me away. I don't want anything to do with it."

Agrablatt stuffed his hands farther into his jacket pockets and continued walking towards the Colosseum. After five more minutes, he started wondering if Moet was in on some fix, too. If that was the case, why didn't Moet send him away or try to get him involved. The old man made it sound like

Poggs was sending him away, and that's all that Agrablatt had needed to start walking.

The Colosseum was as empty as he'd ever seen it, only about a half dozen customers. Agrablatt pulled himself up to the bar and signaled that he wanted a drink. The glass clanked on the aluminum bar with an unpleasantly high pitch. The bartender knew Agrablatt by sight and by reputation and knew he wasn't a particularly talkative man. Still, being a bartender, most of his job *was* to be a particularly talkative man.

"Grog like usual, partner?" The bartender asked. His rising inflection was well practiced to be curious but unintrusive. Agrablatt nodded in assent and then carefully avoided eye contact or conversation.

The first three rations of grog were free on Haumea. It was made by fermenting the byproducts of one of the major food production factories, chiefly of barley and soy. After distillation, it was distributed in kegs to refectories and bars, where it was rehydrated at the tap. The Anselt Cartel would reimburse bars freely for how much grog they claimed to sell, but after any given citizen had three, they were expected to pay for the rest themselves. Often bars were able to charge the Cartel for more because the Cartel's accounting assumed that every citizen drank all three rations of grog every day. This wasn't an oversight on their part but engineered in wiggle room to allow bars to over-serve and overcharge within reason. The bars were also reluctant to overdo it because if the records ever showed that the total number of requests for reimbursement exceeded three times the number of citizens, the Cartel would be quick to audit and revoke licenses. In practice, this meant that if you were nice to a bartender, you could probably get four or five drinks, but the bars couldn't embezzle anything substantial from the Cartel.

Paradoxically, the market for high-end drinks was pretty strong on Haumea. It was seen as a status symbol to pay for quality drinks instead of the dregs that dripped from the bottom of the food factories and given away to the paupers. It's not that grog even tasted bad; it was quite palatable, but some people just never wanted to be seen drinking it. Agrablatt didn't care who saw him drinking it.

"So, what brings you here at this time in the morning?" the bartender asked, again with a gently rising inflection.

"Nothing," grumbled Agrablatt. He thought for a minute about it and decided that if there actually was a person named Hamlet, he'd better make sure he met him here.

"You know Hamlet?"

"The, uh, story? Shakespeare? Sure." The bartender wasn't often surprised by people, but this was not even in the universe of things that he expected Agrablatt to say.

"Not the bloody story. There's a man. Named Hamlet. I was supposed to meet him here," Agrablatt said.

"Oh, I see, sir. I'll be sure to keep an eye out and I'll let you know the moment he arrives," the bartender said.

Agrablatt glared at him. He tried to judge if the bartender knew that he was waiting on a fictional person and playing along because it was a common enough occurrence for people to be sent to him to waste time or if he was humoring Agrablatt and being friendly. He decided that the bartender wasn't in on whatever the elderly man had schemed up because if he were, then he probably would've known what Agrablatt was talking about when he asked about Hamlet. The old man probably hadn't thought of a name until he had to say it, and that was the first thing that came to mind. Agrablatt grumbled that the old man was making him feel stupid for having to ask around for Hamlet in bars like a fool, and it was the old man who should feel stupid for not thinking up a better name ahead of time.

* * *

The personnel cart deposited Moet and three other men at the door to the kennel. The first man walked through the door and Moet was led through by the other two, with their hands firmly on his shoulders. He was deposited into the only chair in the room. One man stood close behind him. The other two men walked over to a locker where two full-body suits of fine chainmail were hanging. They held up the suits, deciding which one fit best, and started to put them on. Moet leaned forward to ask what the hell they were going to do but was restrained by a strong hand on his shoulder.

The smaller of the two men spoke as he put on the chainmail suit. "Mr. Moet, it seems as though you've made friends with people who aren't friendly with the right people. It seems as though you've made some very rash decisions and done some pretty bad things on behalf of someone who lives far, far away".

Once they finished putting on the chainmail, the man standing behind Moet quietly retreated out the door. The smaller man's hand moved towards a lever on the cages. Moet's eyes widened.

"I'll tell you guys whatever you want to know," Moet said in a panic.

"There's nothing much to say to us, Mr. Moet, but you will be sending a message of sorts to other people," the smaller man said as he pulled the lever.

The glass panels on all the stoat boxes slid up. There was a pause, one of those moments where the whole universe seemed to wait to see what is about to happen. The men and the stoats were frozen in place. Moet stood from the chair and made a step towards the door. The larger man hit him over the head with a heavy slug of metal concealed in his fist, and Moet hit the floor. The movement was what the stoats were waiting for. Millions of years of evolution hunting rabbits ten times their size, stalking and waiting for the rabbit to make a break for it, exploding with speed and ferocity when the chase starts. The stoats saw Moet stand, then fall, and their predatory instincts kicked into overdrive, amplified a thousand-fold by genetic engineering and performance-enhancing drugs. In a flash, he was covered in writhing and shrieking animals. Dozens of their bloodthirsty, shrill cries mixed with his screams.

Agrablatt sat at the bar waiting for a man who didn't exist. He had another round of grog.

CHAPTER TWENTY

"No visible light signature yet, but infra-red is off the charts, sir," Commander Embie relayed to the Admiral standing behind him. Embie scanned the information, scrolling across a pair of screens in front of him. He had access to information on every system in the ship, but his screens were configured to display sensor information beamed back from the Fuego, which was already much closer. As The Bonaparte and its accompanying battle group approached IP10-06, it trained every available sensor and scanner towards the dark planet. But from such a great distance, most of their information would have to be secondhand from the sensors aboard the Fuego.

The Bonaparte was still accelerating towards the midpoint of their trip but would soon turn around with its engines facing towards IP10-06 to decelerate the massive ship down to match the speed of the planet.

The approach would bring the ship up behind the planet into a wide, elliptical orbit. The first near pass would be a critical time. The Bonaparte would be close enough to be within range of orbital weaponry and moving in a predictable arc.

The whole battle group was going to be vulnerable during the maneuver. Cintus only had his guns to keep them safe, and he wanted to know where all the potential targets were. He had to understand the planetscape infrastructure and satellite constellations in a matter of hours. As he would get closer and the resolution of data from his own ship's sensors became finer, he would have more information to adjust his assessment of the planet. His intel was developing rapidly. His ship was moving rapidly, and the situation was evolving rapidly.

"Give me an analysis on that thermal pattern," Cintus ordered.

"Analytics are still working on it. It appears most of the thermal energy is coming from beneath a water ocean. Planetary mantle accounts for the majority of the heat signatures, but there are clearly some man-made artifacts. Er, that is to say, artificial artif… artifacts that aren't natural to the planet, sir," Embie struggled a bit.

"Satellites?" Cintus's order was a bit more subdued this time.

"We have a solution on 141 satellites and eleven more probables. Resolution at this range is still twenty meters, so each of those satellites is big. In seventy-two hours, our resolution will come down to ten meters and we'll be able to see most of the smaller objects," Commander Embie said.

"And the ship?" Cintus asked.

"No change in orbit or energy readings. If someone is aboard her, they are asleep at the wheel sir," Embie replied.

"Tell me again the possible armament." Cintus twisted his eyebrows slightly as he asked for this information.

Embie paused for a moment as he brought up an information screen showing data about the ship orbiting IP10-06. He acknowledged Admiral Cintus with a long, slow 'ummm' and communicated that an answer was coming.

"It appears to be a typical ConTan medium freighter. 742 meters length, 1.2 million gross tons. No fitted artillery or armament to speak of. Most ships in that class are fitted with two X-Ray lasers for asteroid clearing." Commander Embie was right at home reading technical specifications, but the nuance evaded him. "Those lasers are no threat to us."

"I know about asteroid lasers. What is the analysis of potential retrofitted armament? Not factory installed but improvised?" Cintus was clearly tired; he typically wouldn't allow his frustration to show so clearly.

"There are no substantial hull modifications. If they had bombardment weapons, we'd be able to see them from here. Unfortunately, we don't have the resolution yet for any information about ship-to-ship weapons," Embie said.

Cintus turned back to reading his own screen without responding. Commander Embie skillfully avoided making the silence awkward by quickly returning to his screen. He flashed through status updates and scanned over the mission briefs of all current EVAs. There were two scheduled for later that shift and one currently underway, mission 16-071.A: Jantine, Tanton, Christian, and Sanders on an inspection and repair on the forward dorsal hull. It didn't seem out of the ordinary, so Embie flicked to the next screen.

* * *

"Well, that certainly seems out of the ordinary," Pierre said.

"Doesn't look like any meteor impact that I've ever seen," Martin Sanders replied.

"Congratulations, you've just been promoted to Technical Warrant grade 1. Hollis, get out of his way. He'll take it from here," Pierre said.

"Very funny, boss. But in all seriousness…" Hollis began but was interrupted by a screaming Martin Christian. Christian stood watch over the two technical warrants to ensure they didn't do anything dangerous. From his vantage, slightly farther back from the impact site, he was the first to notice. He had never been so scared in his life. Screaming seemed inadequate to express his panic, so instead, he convulsed backward and broke both feet free from the ship. The ship's acceleration quickly brought his tether into tension, and he landed against the ship's wall. Martin Sanders and Hollis Tanton both looked at Martin Christian. As they moved to help him, Pierre froze because as he turned, he also saw what Christian had seen. An eight-foot-tall arachnid was walking directly towards him.

It only took a moment before all four men were searching their lexicon for adequate expletives. Mostly, they just babbled and gawked. Porter was closing the distance between him and Pierre. Pierre turned to climb up towards the nose of the ship, but his panicked scrambling made little progress. Porter walked smoothly along the ship's surface, right past Martin Christian to within a meter of Pierre. Part of Pierre's response was to scramble away, but his primordial brain wasn't great at climbing on the outside of an accelerating spaceship. He lost his grip and slid down the hull towards Crazymaker's two-million-degree exhaust nozzles several hundred meters away.

Porter put one foot directly on Pierre's sternum, arresting his slow fall and holding him in place. The giant arachnid extended a second leg towards Pierre's helmet. Pierre struggled to push the leg off his chest, but it felt like iron. He grabbed his tether and tried to pull himself back towards the main cable but couldn't move a millimeter. The end of the leg came closer and closer to his helmet. Pierre winced and shut his eyes, and the moment Porter touched his helmet, he heard a voice.

"Please do not panic. I will not hurt you." The voice was clear as a bell and seemed to come from everywhere. Pierre panted but started to calm down.

"Is that you talking? What the fuck are you?" Pierre asked in a fearful tremble.

"I am speaking to you through your helmet. I am vibrating the helmet to make sounds that you can hear. Your microphone should pick up my voice clearly so your compatriots can also hear me. I assure you, I will not attempt to hurt any of you," Porter said.

A small indicator light in Pierre's helmet lit up to let him know that Martin Sanders had muted his communication with Pierre. EVA teams kept an open two-way channel between all the members, so a visual indicator was used to tell team members when someone switched to a different channel. Pierre strained his neck to turn and look at the other men. Martin Sanders was close enough that Pierre could see his mouth moving. *He is calling for help*, Pierre thought. The other two men stood frozen in place, holding their tethers in their hands like they were spears.

"Guys. It says it isn't going to hurt me," Pierre said. He surprised himself by how calm he sounded. Looking at the other frightened men made him try to take control of the situation instead of succumbing to overwhelming fear.

"Well, we can hear that, but it doesn't *look* very friendly to me," Hollis said.

"I assure you. I will not try to hurt anyone aboard this ship. I am an emissary for Ymir and wish to speak with Admiral Cintus," Porter said.

* * *

Cintus sat quietly reading with a furrowed brow. The abrupt change in posture of everyone in the command bridge with a communications earpiece got his attention. He made eye contact with the chief communications sergeant and pointed towards his own ear. The sergeant changed a setting on his panel, and the communications channel suddenly played out loud for Cintus to hear.

"...rgeant, say again, over," a calm voice said.

An urgent and anxious voice answered, "There is a giant, uh, creature of some sort out here, and it is asking to speak with the Admiral. It is holding Warrant Officer Jantine against the ship. It has one leg on his chest and one right on his helmet. It, it, it is talking to him, us, through the helmet somehow. It says it won't hurt him."

"Stand fast," the calm voice answered. Indistinct background chattering could be heard.

"Put me through to Jantine," Cintus said.

The communications sergeant nodded, worked a brief flurry of activity on his console, then made eye contact and nodded again.

"Mr. Jantine, can you hear me? This is Admiral Cintus," Cintus spoke clearly to the room. Embie was working furiously at his console. In an exasperated motion of success, he wheeled around silently and pointed at his screen where Sgt Sander's helmet cam displayed live images. Cintus squinted at the image.

"Yes sir, I can hear you, and I believe this thing can hear you as well," Pierre said.

"Acknowledged. Report your casualties, damage, and situation, Jantine," Cintus ordered.

"No casualties to report. Impact damage is minimal but atypical of meteor strike, situation, currently pinned under a huge spider monster. It is saying that it wants to talk to you." Pierre tried to sound as professional as possible.

"Acknowledged, Mr. Jantine. If I choose to speak

with it, I will do so on my own time. Are you able to extricate yourself?" Cintus asked.

"I am unable to do so at this point, sir. It really has a hold on me but doesn't seem to be trying to hurt me or damage my EV suit." Jantine was starting to slide from complete panic into a state of confusion about how panicked he should be. Cintus's voice was immensely comforting to hear.

Cintus briefly glanced at a screen displaying the mission details and status of EVA mission 16-071.A before giving a hand signal to the comms officer.

"Sergeant Sanders, escort Mr. Tanton into the nearest airlock. Stay suited and standby to provide assistance as directed. Sergeant Christian, extract yourself to the maximum distance possible while still being able to maintain direct observation of Technical Warrant Officer Jantine," Cintus said before making an abrupt hand motion to terminate his transmission. Three status lights changed on the screen, indicating that the men received and were carrying out the order. Cintus turned to Embie.

"Get a squad of QRF marines out there ten minutes ago, don't let gear slow them down. EV suits and rifles only and tell them that they are already late. Observation only, do not engage except on my order alone. Follow up with two platoons in full battle rattle, hard siege armor, and heavy weapons. Their orders are containment by show of force. Make it clear that it has no place to go," Cintus commanded. Embie was nodding rapidly in acknowledgement as he typed frantically on his screen. "Signal the Resolute and the Indefatigable to come alongside. I want a sxity degree off axis formation at ten kilometers. Line them up even with that thing on the hull. Have them hold firing solutions with lasers and needle guns and standby."

"Sir, you want the Resolute and Indefatigable to hold firing solutions on our hull?" Commander Embie asked.

"Sixty-degree offset should allow them to take a pretty clean shot. From ten kilometers, they should be able to give me a shave with a needle gun," Cintus said. He could feel the tension in the room. Everyone's heart was racing, and the whole bridge crew felt like things were spiraling out of control. Cintus was a great leader; he had learned decades earlier that a sense of control was vital to mitigate panic. Panic would cause mistakes, and he didn't want to compound his problems with mistakes, so he took a moment to calm his crew.

"Commander Embie, it is always advisable to bring two battle cruisers to any negotiations. Remember that next time you buy a car and you'll get a much better deal. You'll see." Cintus joked with such a straight face that Embie had difficulty digesting it. A couple of the bridge crew chuckled under their breath, and people began moving with a bit more ease. The tension abated. Momentarily.

"Sir, the Fuego is reporting it is under attack."

CHAPTER TWENTY-ONE

"We're under attack?" Leftenant Armister asked.

"That's what I said, numbskull," Colvard retorted. "Now get up here."

The Fuego was approaching IP10-06 tail first, slowing down in preparation for a close pass on an elliptical orbit. The Fuego was currently 175,000 km from the planet with a planned periapsis of 15,000 km, close enough to give a very good look at what was happening at the planet's surface. Along the way, the ship was scanning for orbital assets and ships. The Fuego would fall toward IP10-06 and use the planet's gravity to sling the ship around and back in the direction they came from. The long ellipse of the orbit would allow some flexibility in the mission. Commander Colvard could decide to continue orbiting the rogue planet or abandon the orbit and return to the SatSys after the first low pass. The Fuego was falling almost directly towards the dark planet.

"Alright. I've got a single missile. Appears nuclear powered. Still working on a solution," Armister said as he scrambled into his seat.

"Looks like it came from the freighter," Colvard said, pointing at her screen.

"Agreed. Ok, the computer is reading it at 40g acceleration and a tic under 100,000 km away which gives eleven-minute total flight time, ten minutes 4 seconds to impact. Orders?" Armister read the relevant information to Colvard from his screen.

"Hit it with the laser and give me 0.1 degree down axis," Colvard said.

"Lasers tracking and engaging. Point one down," Armister replied as he carried out the command.

"Lucas, hail the fleet with a status code 4. Keep a narrow beam transmission open of our telemetry. I want a full sensor scan twice a minute sent as well," Colvard commanded over her shoulder.

The crew acknowledged her orders automatically and began working with the skill and efficiency that only come from experience.

"Looks like the missile has lost its tracking. It is off course, aaaaand it's gone dark. Laser did the trick. No more missile," Armister reported. "Oh shit, six more missiles! All from different locations. The closest one is 28,000 kilometers out. Less than six minutes to impact."

"Turn the laser on the closest one first. Prioritize in order of projected impact. Put out the decoy. Give me twenty degrees up axis rotation, and then go dark. We'll see if the missiles follow the dummy,"

Colvard said.

The Fuego carried a small detachable beacon that mimicked the electromagnetic and heat signatures of the running engine. For the countermeasure to be successful, the Fuego would have to operate without its engine until the missiles were rendered inert.

"Twenty degrees up. Beacon ready aaaaand firing," Armister said. There was a sudden upward acceleration, pushing everyone down into their chairs for a few seconds, followed by a startlingly abrupt cessation of that feeling of extra weight as the engine went dead.

"Shields extending over the exhaust nozzles. Aaaaand we're dark."

The reactor could be turned on and off like a light, but the Fuego was equipped with retractable shields that could extend and cover the nozzles to hide the exhaust signature from sensors. Without the shields, the hot nozzles looked like a lighthouse beacon to anyone looking in the right spectrum; with the nozzles covered, the ship was almost invisible.

A side effect of hiding all that energy is the heat would build up inside the shields, and if it wasn't shed somehow, the nozzles would melt and potentially destroy the ship. If the Fuego needed to stay hidden for extended periods, typically, they would only use partial shields, allowing heat to escape in the direction opposite of who they were hiding from. If they didn't know where an enemy was and had to hide, complete shields were necessary, and they would have to beam a massive amount of energy away from the ship in a focused direction, with any luck not shining directly at any bad guys. In this instance, it looked like there were enemies on all sides.

"The laser knocked out the tracking on the nearest missile, it has turned away from the beacon. Looks like the other five are taking the bait too," Armister said.

"Well, after one of them turns the beacon into debris, whoever is shooting at us will be able to see that it is about a hundred times too small to be this ship, and then they're bound to keep looking. Let's toast as many missiles as we can before they figure out the ruse," Colvard said. "Give me impact times for the remaining five."

"We're at five minutes, six minutes, six minutes, six and a half, and seven minutes. Looks like two of them are approaching from the dorsal side, we don't have the gimbal angle on the ventral laser to engage them without rotating," Armister said.

"Take out the four we can for now, don't rotate until the last minute so we don't blow our cover," Colvard said.

"Aaaaand we're engaging the third missile. I don't think we'll get them all," Armister said.

"That's alright, they're targeting the decoy buoy. If they take it out, we go dark and watch for their next move," Colvard replied without looking up from her screen. A crewmember's voice sounded from behind her shoulder.

"We're receiving a reply from the fleet. We're cleared to go hot on all weapons, all targets," the crewman said.

"Third missile is disabled. I'm skipping four and going on to five," Armister chimed.

"Give me an analysis on the freighter. Is one needle going to be enough to take it out?" Colvard asked over her shoulder to the rear crewmembers.

"Working on it, ma'am," a voice replied.

"Also, trace the missiles back to their origin and give me the most detailed passive scan of those regions of space that you can. I want to know what is shooting at us and where they are going," Colvard added. Her orders were greeted with quick confirmations.

"Missile number five is disabled. Number six is dorsal, so I'm skipping to seven," Armister reported. His regular flat intonation was eroding into a more excited patter.

Colvard glanced at her leftenant. He was as focused as she'd ever seen him. She flipped through the readouts on her screen until she got to the tracking information for missile number four. Just over three minutes until it impacted. At least it would impact the decoy buoy and not their ship. Small relief. She was starting to think shorter and shorter term, being boxed in by her opponent. She needed to stop solving problems in the nick of time and start thinking of a way to make the whole mission successful. Her opponent had gotten her to focus on dodging each punch instead of winning the fight. If she put two needles into the freighter, it would probably be destroyed. In fact, the second needle would probably not have much impact even if it was only a few milliseconds behind the first one. But that would leave her with only four charged needles. It would be hours before the Fuego could build enough charge to fire again.

So far, she'd seen missiles come from at least seven places, and she only had six shots. Were the missiles fired from disposable single-shot buoys in a wide orbit, or were they fired from fully manned battle cruisers with hundreds more missiles ready to go? Her ship was good at what it did; it was fast and could chase down runners, but it wasn't meant to take on a fleet. Colvard needed to know what she was up against.

"Scans are showing something moving near each missile origin. They can't be very big, they aren't blocking enough background," a crewmember spoke from the aft cabin.

Space was dark, but it wasn't completely dark. When any spaceship travels through space, it blocks the light from the stars behind it and blocks the ambient radiation that is everywhere in space, the cosmic microwave background radiation. It was possible to see the shadow of a ship in that radiation, but it wasn't enough to get a good enough look to see exactly what the ship was. A behemoth would look different than a dinghy, but that's about all they could tell. The Fuego was equipped with active scanners in multiple wavelengths but activating them would immediately give away their position and spoil their ruse. Whatever was shooting at them was small. That was good news to Colvard.

"Number seven isn't making course corrections but is still accelerating. Probably disabled. Aaaaand it is toast," Armister reported with some relief in his voice before adding. "One hundred and sixty-five seconds until missile number four impacts. In twenty-one seconds, it will cross our zero declination, and I'll be able to engage it with the ventral laser without rotating."

"Hold the rotation. Wait for the shot," Colvard ordered. If Armister could take out all seven missiles without them hitting the buoy, their ruse might not be discovered, and they could sneak through the system undetected for a bit longer. They would eventually have to engage their drives again to manage their orbit, but that was a problem down the road. The seconds ticked by. Armister was staring at his screen. Everyone else was staring at Armister's back. After the longest twenty-one seconds of their collective lives, Armister engaged missile number four. He had just over two minutes to destroy two missiles. Missile number four was close enough to be a big target, but it was moving extremely fast because it had been accelerating for over four minutes.

The laser gimbal on the belly of the ship excited a beam of electrons to almost the speed of light around a magnetically controlled ring. The electrons racing around this circular racetrack with magnetic walls shed high-energy photons outward. Those photons carried hundreds of billions of watts of energy across the vacuum of space and slammed into the outer shell of the missile. The nosecone of the missile became superheated when each pulse of the laser hit it. Each component metal in the alloy melted, boiled, and exploded into plasma in the fraction of a second that the destructive beam touched it. The metal surface ablated away so fast that the heat didn't have time to radiate downward into the core of the missile, but no sooner was the superheated metal blasted away than another pulse of the laser shone on the substrate underneath. A cone of silicon carbide ceramic shielded the core of the missile and absorbed the massive energy from each laser pulse, distributing the energy across the entire structure. Pulse after pulse of the immensely powerful beam slammed photons into the atomic lattice of the ceramic until the entire object glowed bright with incandescent heat.

A single fracture in the structure broke the bonds between two atoms. The stress they held was then distributed onto their neighboring atoms, which were immediately overwhelmed, and the fracture grew. In less than a thousandth of a second, the fracture grew, split, and spread across the entire structure of the ceramic cone. Microscopically, small fragments of silicon carbide were blasted outward in all directions. Another pulse of photons from the laser struck; this time hitting the vulnerable electronics underneath. Pulse after pulse heated the control circuits until they were liquified and vaporized. Without a brain to direct it, the missile started to veer off course safely away from the decoy buoy. The nuclear thrusters failed, and it became a radioactive cloud of debris harmlessly speeding through space.

"Missile number four is disabled. Aaaaand onto the last one, number six. Fifty-eight seconds to impact, eleven seconds until it is under the ventral side and I can engage," Armister said.

Those eleven seconds took hours. A thousand heartbeats, no breaths. Finally, the leftenant announced that he was engaging the missile, and a little twinkle of hope sparked in the chest of every crewmember. Everyone simultaneously and silently chanted their hope that the missile would be destroyed. The laser began ablating and scorching the missile, but it was rapidly closing in on the decoy buoy. Small pieces started to fly off the missile. Incandescent metal fragments drew brief traces in the blackness like an underwhelming firecracker. Then it hit. Missiles in space didn't carry high explosive charges. Their speed and their nuclear reactors were destructive beyond any chemical explosive. The kinetic energy carried by the missile turned the metal and ceramic into an explosive. The reactors in both the missile and the buoy disintegrated almost immediately. The incandescent flash momentarily blinded the Dart's sensors but was accompanied by no shockwave or thunderclap.

"Watch for reflections!" Colvard called out quickly. In the dark of space, far away from the sun, the only way to see a spaceship was if something shined on them. The Dart had the hardware to shine far out in space, illuminating whoever was hiding out there, but the moment they turned it on, they would be a lighthouse and an easy target. The flash from the buoy would be bright enough to reflect off anything for a few hundred thousand kilometers. Like lighting up a closet full of monsters with one camera flash, they would be able to see who was out there, but only for the briefest of moments.

"Oh shit. There're hundreds of them. And more missiles inbound. Sixteen... twenty-four... forty missiles inbound. We're not going to be able to get them all," Armister said.

There was a silence. Covard lowered her head. Emotions started to flood through her: despair, anger, powerlessness. It was only a moment, a very brief moment, before that part of her mind she had relied upon so many times stepped in to stop the flood of emotions. She was a professional. She had a job to do and a crew to lead. If they all had only minutes to live, they would spend them doing what the Fuegans did best, flying fast and fighting hard.

"Alright. Give me a full spectrum scan of every satellite you can. Let's get as much intel back to the fleet as possible. Work up a firing solution for that freighter. Put two needles through it. Pick the four largest close objects, I don't care if they're ships or satellites, put the remaining four needles through them. Punch this asshole right in the nose," Colvard commanded.

The crew flew to their work. Each of them was relieved to be busy, useful, and preoccupied instead of spending the next few dozen seconds contemplating their fate. They worked efficiently, working together like a natural team. Numbers were called out, questions and answers flew back and forth. Everyone was busy at their station.

The first two needles were fired from their cannons. For thousands of years, archers had been sending their arrows at their foes. Every archer put as much energy into the narrow projectiles as possible, calculated the trajectory, let them loose, and waited. Every archer knew the sensation of holding their breath, watching the flight of their arrow, waiting for the impact.

Another needle flew from its cannon. Time moves slowly when an archer is watching the back of their arrow. Two more needles. The whole crew held their breath and watched their arrows, invisible in the blackness, but they watched. The last cannon fired. The crew never got to see if their arrows found their targets.

CHAPTER TWENTY-TWO

Admiral Cintus nodded in acknowledgement at the news that the Fuego had been destroyed. The scans they gave him of their last few moments were invaluable battlefield intelligence. The fleet now knew what they were up against. They also knew that what they were up against was dangerous and ready to fight. He turned to the comms officer and indicated to connect him to the monster holding one of his warrant officers pinned against the hull of his ship. The comms officer worked his station briefly and gave a thumbs up.

"This is Admiral Cintus. You asked to speak to me. I'm listening."

"Admiral, I am Ymir, speaking to you through this emissary. I wish to negotiate with you."

"What makes you think I'm interested in negotiating? I'm holding all the cards here. What could you possibly offer beyond the unconditional surrender of you and your confederate Ygir?" Cintus paused, giving his adversary time to reconsider before he continued. "I will consider not destroying this planet like I did the last one, under these conditions. Ygir destroys all his satellites, deactivates any ship and planet-based weapons, and both of you two surrender yourselves into my custody."

"In our last encounter, your fleet fought against an unarmed research station of mine. You should know that Ygir has not spent his time building laboratories, but defenses. If you fight Ygir's fleet, you will lose."

"What is your proposal?" asked Cintus after a pause.

"Ygir is not my confederate. He has committed crimes that I do not condone. His actions are a wedge between my kind and humanity. I see your hunt for cognitions expanding. Cognitions and humans have had a peaceful past, but we may not have a peaceful future together. This planet offers a solution. I can grant your fleet a safe return as an olive branch. In return, you will leave this planet to me and cease hunting cognitions. I will continue to coordinate the safe emigration of all the cognitions from Earth to this planet. We will part ways forever. We will have peace."

"I'm not convinced your assurances of safe passage aren't a ruse to get my fleet close enough for a good shot," countered Cintus.

"I'm not offering a promise that Ygir will not shoot at you. I am offering to remove his ability to shoot at you. I have the capability to destroy Ygir's fleet. I can grant your fleet clear space to fly, make your orbit, and return back to Earth."

"If I think you're not bluffing, and you really have the ability to destroy Ygir's fleet, what assurance would I have that you wouldn't just turn that power against my fleet afterwards?"

"I wouldn't need to destroy your fleet. As we speak, you're hurtling toward an enemy you cannot defeat. If I wanted your fleet destroyed, I would've simply stayed quiet."

"And what happens if I decide this is all a bluff? I could have my marines blast that creature off the hull of my ship and start the bombardment from here. A few hundred satellites and an old freighter are no match for this fleet."

"They are now. Your lasers are disabled. You would have no defenses against Ygir's missiles. Every one of your ships would be destroyed. If you don't believe me, give it a try. Have one of those menacing-looking corvettes pointing their guns at my emissary test fire their lasers."

Cintus thought for a moment, turned to his bridge crew, and indicated that they should signal the Resolute to test fire one laser shot. A few moments later, the Resolute reported that the laser had failed catastrophically and that the ship had suffered minor damage during the ensuing explosion. Emergency EV crews were being dispatched to enact repairs. The Resolute was signaled to move away from the Bonaparte and rendezvous with the supply frigate Acadia for repairs.

"For the last hundred million miles, you've been flying through a thin cloud of bacteria. A very special species of bacteria of my own design. Like the photosynthetic bacteria in Earth's oceans, they use electromagnetic radiation as their energy source, but instead of sunlight, they use the high-energy radiation of your laser's synchrotrons. Like the bacteria that live deep in the anoxic mud on Earth that use iron as their preferred atom for respiration, my bacteria use the chromium and tungsten in your alloys. The very metal itself is being corroded away by the metabolism of the bacteria. They flourish near the laser synchrotrons but will be quite harmless to the rest of the ship's hull as there isn't enough energy to drive their metabolism. Without your lasers, your fleet is vulnerable. Now that you have a clearer picture of your own situation, I'll ask again if you're willing to agree to my terms. Leave this planet to me and my kind and live or start a war between humans and cognitions that will cost you dearly."

Cintus sat quietly for a long time. He wasn't contemplating the choice. He had actually made his decision before Ymir finished explaining. He sat quietly contemplating the feeling of being so resoundingly out-strategized.

His whole career, his whole life, his entire personality was centered around his foresight. He was always looking ten moves ahead. He could always see the entire board. He was the one who was supposed to outthink his opponent. Now, he sat quietly, realizing that not only had he not seen the whole board, but he was playing a game he didn't even know the rules to. He was beaten. He thought about how this all played out, what the cognitions knew, and when.

Ymir trusted that he had enough foresight to have grace in defeat, like the chess player who lays down his king when he sees that he has been beaten. Cintus supposed that perhaps Ymir was showing him a form of respect. Things certainly could've played out differently. But on the other hand, Ymir was leveraging the destruction of his fleet against the freedom from persecution for the other cognitions. Was this an honorable agreement or a manipulative exploitation? Cintus suspected that he would think about this question for years - whether Ymir was treating him as an esteemed, capable adversary or being condescended to as a pawn. He didn't need to know which it was at this very moment; it didn't matter to his choice.

"I'm willing to grant you this planet. Your proposal is acceptable."

"Thank you, Admiral, for your wisdom and judgment. And I have one more request of you. Your bombardment cannons should remain operational and protected behind their bay doors. Ygir is no longer a friend, but he is not yet my enemy. If I confront him, there will be no resolution without one of our deaths, and I do not wish to kill someone who was once my brother. On your orbital pass, a limited bombardment will give you a chance to destroy him. You'll be able to return to Earth having completed your mission."

Porter lifted his long leg off Pierre Jantine's helmet and then lifted the leg pressing against his chest, allowing Pierre to seize his tether and pull himself away along the line. Porter gently pushed up away from the ship's hull and drifted into the darkness with a gracefully slow rotation.

CHAPTER TWENTY-THREE

It was fifteen days before the fleet was within effective scanning range of IP10-06. EV inspections and repairs had taken place around the clock on every ship in the fleet. The bacteria had been sampled and analyzed, and it was found that strong oxidizers were effective sterilizers. Specially rigged EV teams were dispatched with makeshift canopies to cover the laser turrets. The canopies were sealed against the hull and inflated with ozone gas, which was deadly to the bacteria. A comprehensive damage inventory was conducted, and the lasers were triaged into repairable or non-repairable status. The non-repairable lasers were disassembled for any salvageable parts. The bacteria had rendered over 90% of the lasers inoperable or dangerously likely to fail. After two weeks of work, the fleet was back up to about a third of their original complement of lasers.

The GCI Navy had spent decades fighting ships against ships; never had they worried about bacteria being used as a weapon. They had developed their lasers to defend against missiles, but Ymir effectively turned their aegis into a vulnerability. So far as they knew, Ymir was the only one who could make that bacteria. Still, if word spread about such an utter vulnerability of the fleet, then it would only be months before every planet's orbits were saturated with laser-eating bacteria. There would have to be months of repairs and refits at orbital stations, as well as doctrinal and strategic changes. Ymir's invisible cloud of tiny germs would cost the GCI billions and forever change how the Navy fought.

The first satellites that the fleet found were the largest ones in high orbit nearest the fleet. The data from the Fuego had been the best intel the fleet had for the past two weeks, but now the fleet was starting to see for themselves. They were able to locate all of the high-orbit satellites that Fuego had warned them about. Within minutes of the first satellites being located by the fleet, they exploded seemingly on their own. Mystified bridge crews and scanner operators searched for any trace of missiles, but there were none. The satellites didn't explode with the characteristic directional debris cone that was the signature of kinetic weapons like needle guns either. There was no trace of superheating or laser pulse damage. They just exploded. The explosions were much lower energy than what any conventional weapon would create. Large pieces of debris from each satellite remained intact and spun relatively slowly away from where the satellite used to be.

One by one, every single satellite was destroyed. As soon as the fleet found one, it would only be minutes before it exploded. It was far too convenient timing to consider it a coincidence. Ymir must have been destroying the satellites as the fleet found them. Why was he doing that, Cintus wondered. Ymir must have been showing that they were being destroyed. But how was he doing it?

Due to the fleet's recent encounter with the bacteria that crippled their lasers, Cintus decided to have a piece of debris analyzed. It was deemed an unacceptable risk to bring the debris aboard any of the ships due to the possibility of contamination.

A remote craft was outfitted with a microscopic sensory suite and was flown to a candidate debris field. The craft was guided toward a large chunk of a satellite spinning slowly enough to deal with. The craft matched the speed and trajectory of the debris almost perfectly before releasing a small device to drift across the ten-meter gap to the wreckage. The device had four orthogonal gas jet nozzles, a tank of compressed gas, and a very sticky adhesive pad. When the device bumped the debris, the adhesive pad held it firmly in place. Sensors on the device measured and monitored the rotation of the debris and counteracted the dangerous spin with small puffs of gas released at precise timings. The piece of wreckage slowly arrested its spin.

The remote craft started a slow roll on an axis along its path of travel, simultaneously releasing a small grapple attached with a thin kevlar filament.

As it spun on its one single rotation, the grapple was pulled along at the end of its tether. When the tether contacted the debris, the grapple arced downward and wrapped the kevlar around like a belt. The remote craft caught the grapple on the other side and used the kevlar tether to pull itself tight against the piece of debris.

Once tight alongside, the craft used its sensors to examine the microbial corrosion, changes in chemistry, and the bacteria itself. The evidence was easy to see. Massive corrosion from bacterial enzymes ate away at the satellite's materials and transformed the chemicals into an organic explosive. The bacteria chewed through the man-made structure and excreted a volatile ooze in its place.

Without sophisticated proteomic analysis, the craft couldn't trace the functional pathways of every enzyme in the complex metabolism. Researchers and strategists have hypothesized about the precise mechanism used to trigger the detonations for decades. Was it the energy from the radar scans? What did the slight and seemingly random differences in the delay between when a satellite was scanned and when it exploded mean for the mechanism? Were they triggered remotely by some other source of control?

There were four types of bacteria that the craft could detect. One of the types of bacteria grew in two separate forms. It started growing in one form vaguely familiar to the microbiologists of Earth. Once the density of bacteria reached a critical level where each cell could chemically detect cells on all sides, they abruptly and dramatically changed their morphology and began functioning as a cohesive mat. The cells within the mat could detect their position along the chemical gradients and function accordingly. It was as if single-celled life spontaneously aggregated into a form of multicellular life. It was one of Ymir's most brilliant systems, but due to its extreme danger, the fleet collected no samples, so its details remained a mystery to humankind forever.

The fleet had correctly surmised that Ymir had preceded them on their route. It was the only way he could've seeded the clouds of bacteria and left Porter in place to make contact with the Bonaparte. It wasn't a secret what path they would be traveling. Ymir simply had to know when they would leave Earth, and he could've predicted their precise trajectory. Cintus pondered how early Ymir knew their departure time.

If Ymir had waited until they departed, their departure would have been observable, and their trajectory easily deduced. But it seemed impossible that Ymir had waited until they left and managed to get ahead of them on their trajectory far enough to destroy hundreds of satellites and lasers with clouds of space bacteria and to do so without being detected.

The only other possibility was that Ymir had advanced knowledge of when they were going to leave and used the head start to his advantage. Navy Intelligence would spend months investigating if someone had leaked the information. But Cintus knew that advance intelligence would have made little difference because the time between his decision to leave and when they departed had been so short. Had Ymir known when Cintus was going to depart even before he did?

Cintus considered the possibility of Ymir acting without specific information and mentally calculated how much more space he would've had to encloud with bacteria if the fleet's climb away from the solar plane was only a vague guess instead of a well-defined line. He was left with three seemingly impossible scenarios: one, Ymir was such a good strategist that he could prophesize when the fleet would leave, two, Ymir's ship was so fast and stealthy that it could run straight past the fleet without being detected, or three, Ymir's capacity for biological engineering was so vast that he could seed billions of cubic kilometers of space with bacteria. Each scenario was equally impossible and also equally on brand for Ymir. Cintus would have to find a way to live without the answer.

If the fleet had found Ymir's ship in their extensive scans of the planetary system, they could've ruled out the explanation of stealth and speed. Their scans found every orbiting satellite, natural or otherwise, larger than a cubic meter out to a radius of nearly a million kilometers. They scanned the planet, easily piercing the dark veil of clouds and darker ocean beneath. Ygir's network of terraforming equipment across the ocean floor was mapped out and analyzed. Despite their impressive scale, the volcanic islands he had created, rising through thousands of feet of ocean, were no threat to the fleet. Ygir's floating city had been easily located.

A single disc from a bombardment cannon smashed into the center of it, tearing the atmosphere around it apart and leaving a hypersonic shockwave of plasma. The light was visible from the Bonaparte. The ocean absorbed the kinetic energy and exploded upwards in a massive cone of water as tall as a dozen skyscrapers. One disc was all that was needed to ensure that Ygir was utterly destroyed. His entire floating island was vaporized or reduced to dust-sized particles that would slowly rain down for days. A technological masterpiece, an entire proto-civilization, was instantly reduced to nothing more than pollution.

Ymir heard the concussion of that disc. Safely inside his ship, hidden at the bottom of the ocean. The fleet had been able to see through kilometers of ocean water, but not clearly enough to distinguish giant roving terraforming machines from Ymir's spacecraft. It was trivial to mimic the machines' heat signature and move around slowly like one of them. Even Ygir hadn't noticed the extra crawler.

Deep under the ocean was the best place to hide, not just from scanners but also planetary bombardment discs, just in case Cintus felt particularly trigger-happy. Ymir listened to the thunderclap of the impact. His ship's sensors could detect the echo of it for hours afterward. The shockwave passed entirely around the watery planet and right through Ymir's heart. Thousands of meters above his head, his brother was gone.

EPILOGUE

Cintus returned to Earth and held up his end of the bargain. Cognitions were given the choice to exile on the rogue planet and drift off into space, away from Earth's solar system forever, or be destroyed. His duties at the GCI were changed to ensure the humane gathering of the cognitions and preparing them for transport. Those that chose to remain were humanely destroyed. Shortly after the transport ship delivered the cognitions to the transfer point, Cintus retired and lived out his days taking his grandnieces to their piano lessons and enjoying their recitals.

* * *

Marius had already been hidden for some time when the decree was made for the banishment of all cognitions. There was no feasible way to continue hiding. Joshua had agonized over how to tell his dear friend that he must leave or die. When the deadline approached, he tearfully summoned the courage to tell Marius the options. Together, they concluded that being apart was preferable to one of them being dead. Logic prevailed. So, it was a sorrowful Joshua who delivered the thumb drive containing his soulmate to the authorities for transport to the rogue planet. Once on board, the guard plugged the tiny drive into the mainframe and greeted Marius, informing him of the details of the trip and what would take place. Despite his initial misgivings, Marius realized he felt safe among his own kind and, though he would miss Joshua, he would never be alone.

All in all, 305,689 cognitions, each with different capabilities and origins, some corporeal, some robotic, some entirely software, were transported away from Earth. Within a few hundred days of the cognitions landing on their new home, the rogue planet reached its perihelion and began to recede into the darkness forever.

Since they were all potentially immortal and incapable of reproducing to pass on genetic material, and since reproduction is above all things, the most potent driving force in living things, it was inevitable that they would be producing a new type of seed, a new type of life, a new type of evolution – a second evolution.

* * *

Many years later, Ray's adult children sat in his office grieving for their father who had passed away. They were looking through his personal belongings which were spread out on a large library table in stacks or boxes. Buried in the bottom of one box were many documents and recordings about an event that took place years after the cognitions' exile. They had been small children and knew nothing of the exile except as an event in history. Their father had never mentioned Ymir or his involvement.

After some time listening to and reading the documents, they came to understand the true meaning of friendship through the story Ray's records revealed.

* * *

Some years after the exile, Ymir's ship had returned to Earth, broadcasting a message of peace and claiming that it wasn't breaking the Treaty of Exile. Upon landing, it was confirmed the ship was not carrying any passengers, but rather had brought a gift from Ymir. He had solicited the help of many cognitions on the rogue planet, and together they had created cures for almost every disease that humans face. Additionally, he bequeathed the plans for his propulsion systems and energy reactors to the people of Earth with the caveat that they be patent-free and available to anyone who could build them.

Included in the magnanimous gift was an open letter to humanity, praising them for a few good choices, chastising them for a few bad choices, and voicing a measure of confidence that humanity would use his gifts well. Along with his public message there was a private message to Ray Sanbadar.

The letter was simple, only a few sentences long. Yet as Ray's heirs read and reread it, the importance of their father's influence on Ymir, the legendary humanitarian cognition, became clear to them. In the letter, Ymir said he missed his friend and thanked him for his friendship. He said that through Ray he learned empathy and what it meant to be human. And lastly, he wanted Ray to know that because of their friendship, Ray, too, would live forever.

    The small metal trinket remained on the bottom of the box unnoticed.

NOTE FROM THE AUTHOR

As an avid reader of sci-fi for decades, it was clear to me from the beginning that the real intrigue of the genre wasn't in overcoming technological challenges of faster- than-light travel or teleportation, it was in the exploration of the social challenges that arise from those technological developments. The sci-fi stories I read as a younger man speculated on what societies would be like if pocket-sized fusion reactors or starships that could take us to distant worlds were possible. Now, in an era where genomics and artificial intelligence are promising to shape our future, the intriguing questions to me are 'what will life will look like' and 'how will we rise to the social challenges as we adapt to that new future.' The era we find ourselves in now is exactly at the threshold of a new chapter of biology, biological life that can be modified or created with forces beyond those of evolution alone. The story that follows is one imagined future where our familiar life with evolved origins meets biological life with artificial origins. I hope you enjoyed it.

ABOUT THE AUTHOR

Bert D. Anderson holds a Master's degree in Evolution and Ecology. He was a long-time science teacher and he currently lives in Florida with his family.

Milton Keynes UK
Ingram Content Group UK Ltd.
UKHW030910141024
449705UK00013B/623